JETT & LEIGHTON

On Cravenwood Block

A.D. ELLIS

A.D. ELLIS

ONE

Jett Elijah Nelson

"HEY, SWEET CHEEKS," he said as he sashayed his way to the counter in my new tattoo shop. "Brought you a coffee." His smile lit up the front foyer space of Cravin' Ink Designs and his gray eyes twinkled as he handed me the travel cup.

Leighton had been coming into my tattoo shop every day since I'd hung my open sign. For two weeks, the flashy blond had shown up, spewing ridiculous pet names and bringing coffee concoctions sweet enough to rot my teeth.

He'd pop in, flirt and drop off coffee, chit chat about tattoos he'd like to get, and then wave goodbye.

From his artfully-styled, purposely-floppy blond hair to his ever-changing eye-catching earrings to his colorful nails, Leighton was a tiny hurricane blowing through my life every single day.

Disruptive and inconvenient, for sure.

Left me a bit discombobulated after he whirled away.

But also kinda refreshing in a weird way—like he blew away the debris in my life.

Despite my attempts to remain my usual closed-off, disconnected, aloof self, I discovered I actually began to anticipate his daily arrival. Leighton's visits almost had a grounding effect on me.

Like a visit from a good friend.

Which was insane.

I didn't really do the whole friend thing. Never had.

Not that I didn't *want* friends, I just didn't really connect with people that well.

Sure, in high school, I'd had a group of people I sometimes hung out with. Mostly parties here and there, the occasional study group, maybe grabbing a bite to eat if our schedules happened to be the same.

But I didn't consider them friends.

Girlfriends had come and gone back then. Sex was decent, but they always moved on when they finally got tired of me never opening up.

What was wrong with someone keeping to themselves? Why did I need to spill my guts to strangers?

If you let people in a bit more, they wouldn't be strangers, would they?

Whatever.

Letting people in made me anxious.

I had exactly one close relationship in my life and that was with Grandpa Nelson.

It wasn't like I purposely avoided making friends, I just didn't know how to have them while still keeping them at arm's length. So, I allowed people to think I was intimidating—dark hair, dark eyes, a bit of brooding, and a shit ton of tattoos made that part easy—went about my solo life, and didn't let myself think about what it might be like to have a big group of friends.

Which was why Leighton's sudden and now-seemingly-constant presence in my life was throwing me for a loop.

It should have irritated me.

It should have made me itchy and had me doing my best to avoid him or push him away.

But it didn't.

And that was weird.

I didn't hate it.

I didn't understand it.

But I wasn't sure I wanted to question it too much.

Leighton would likely get tired of me being a bit stand-offish and find someone chattier and more sociable soon.

"Stop calling me those stupid names," I groused, taking the coffee cup from him, and tossing the toothpick from between my teeth into the trashcan—I'd stopped smoking years ago, and the toothpick helped ease the need I still got from time-to-time. "Thanks." I knew refusing the drink would end up with him just leaving it on the counter. Taking a sip, I winced.

"What?" Leighton asked.

"If you're going to insist on coming in here with coffee every damn day, could you at least bring the real stuff and not this syrupy crap?" I'd given up on thinking he'd just stop coming in because I wanted him to. Leighton was the quintessential dog with a bone and for some reason he'd chosen me to fixate on.

Flipping his silky blond hair from his even prettier

eyes, Leighton bit the corner of his lip and grinned mischievously. "So, you're saying you like me coming here every day?"

I couldn't help the laugh that escaped me. It felt good. I didn't laugh a lot.

Don't get me wrong. I was content with my life. My art was at its best yet. My new tattoo shop—thanks to Grandpa's generous gift—was up and running. Maybe not making bank yet, but I had to be patient.

I'd escaped my overbearing, never-satisfied, constantly-demanding-more parents when I moved out at eighteen. Living with Grandpa had been a nice reprieve, and I knew he'd let me stay for as long as I needed, but getting a place closer to my shop was the plan. Eventually.

"What part of *bring me decent coffee* sounded like *I like you coming here every day?*" I asked, unable to control the smirk fighting to play at my lips.

"Sweetheart, you're new here. Just consider me the friendly Cravenwood boy." Leighton spoke the words innocently enough, but the innuendo was clear.

I snorted. "The Cravenwood boy, huh?"

"Obviously," Leighton said with a wink. "Aren't we all cravin' wood?"

I shook my head and rolled my eyes, ignoring his comment. "Where'd the name Cravenwood come from anyway?" All I really knew about the two-block location on the west side of Midtown was it was kinda a community within a community.

Leighton grinned, clearly pleased to have a reason to stay and keep chatting. He leaned his five-foot-eight-ish frame against the glass display case counter—eventually, I hoped to have a piercer on-site and feature available hardware for sale in the case.

"Well, my understanding is that about twenty-five years ago, a guy named Robert Cravenwood was angry about the planned demolition of buildings and subsequent construction of a parking garage." Leighton tapped a bright pink nail on the glass. "He bought the buildings and the land—can we say total sugar daddy?—restored a few buildings, rebuilt a few, and brought this area back to life—Cravenwood was born. It's not an actual town, but Midtown named the road running down the middle of these two blocks Cravenwood Avenue, and a lot of the businesses that popped up soon after worked Cravenwood or *craving* into their name somehow."

"Cravenwood Apartments, Cravenwood Education Center, Cravenwood Tap, Cravings bakery, Cravin'-a-Cup coffee shop," I said, listing many of the businesses I'd noticed around the area.

"Yep." Leighton popped his *p*. "Even Cravin' Ink Designs kept with the trend."

My new shop was a small building originally designed as something else, but it had been a tattoo shop for at least three years from my understanding.

"Yeah, I don't hate the name, so I decided to keep it for now."

"I guess you don't *have* to, but it works and fits with the names of so many other businesses around here." Leighton shrugged. "The pet store, diner, hair stylist, grocery, and flower shop all went with the more boring Cravenwood Grocery or Cravenwood Diner. Not *as* creative as some of the others, and I suppose the names could be changed depending on the owner, but they get the point across. Our little area is a bit like a bubble inside a bubble." He gestured toward the door and bright afternoon sun. "Midtown isn't super large, I'd say it borders right at the edge of a large town and a small city, but living and working in Cravenwood makes everything feel smaller, safer, and somehow more connected."

"You live here? In the apartments?" I'd been looking at the Cravenwood apartments online, but the site said only a waiting list was available. I'd enjoyed living with my grandpa for the past seven years, but at twenty-five-years-old—and now owning a business thirty minutes away from Grandpa's house—moving to Cravenwood, or at least close by, made more sense.

Leighton smiled broadly. "I do. Are you looking for a place?"

"Yeah. I'd love to get into those apartments. Do you know how long the waiting list is? What's the rent like?"

"Baby cakes, you let Leighton do his thing, and I'll have you in a lease and moving in by the end of the week."

"What? How?" My little hurricane was making no sense.

Jesus, Nelson, stop thinking about this guy as yours. You're not even gay. What the hell's gotten into you?

"Let's just say I've got connections." Leighton checked his phone. "I better go, but I'll stop in tomorrow and give you more details. I'm working a double shift today at the coffee shop, stop in if you take a break and want a pretty face to stare at for a while."

I grabbed a toothpick from one of the boxes I kept all

over the shop. A lot of tattoo artists took smoke breaks. Me? I kept the cravings at bay with tiny shards of wood between my teeth. "You really need to work on your gaydar and your self-esteem."

Leighton laughed, all throaty and flirty. "My self-esteem has no issues and my gaydar is fully-functioning. In fact, even my bi-sight is twenty-twenty."

The little shit winked, waved, and sauntered his lean frame out the door with his ass looking sinful in a pair of faded skinny jeans.

His bi-sight? And since when did I notice other guys' asses?

What the actual fuck was going on?

Hurricane Leighton had once again wreaked havoc and left me to sort through the rubble.

How did one guy—yeah, a pretty, slim, flashy, persistent guy, but still, a guy all the same—pop up and get me all twisted up?

I'd never been as addled over anyone before.

No girl had ever gotten under my skin this way. I couldn't remember a single break-up I'd actually been upset over.

No guy had ever even tried—at least that I could recall. Maybe I'd been oblivious, or too busy trying to keep my distance, but I don't think guys had ever flirted with me. True, a lot of people gave me a wide berth due to their assumption I was scary, but I still didn't think I would have missed guys flirting with me.

So, what was it about Leighton that had him working his way under my skin after just two weeks of annoying me daily?

Maybe you're just curious about the apartment situation he mentioned.

Yeah, maybe that was it.

My inner thoughts scoffed at me.

Pftt, right. Because he hadn't been working his way under your skin long *before he mentioned the apartments?*

Shut up.

Gnawing on the toothpick, I did my best to push all thoughts of Leighton from my mind. I had appointments coming up and pieces to work on before the clients arrived. I didn't need my head all wrapped up in a flirty pretty-boy who smelled of dark roast and cinnamon sunshine.

Checking through the appointment book, I sighed heavily.

I most definitely needed to get my head a lot more wrapped around the fact that my appointments were slim-to-none.

I'd known coming into this business adventure that the prior shop artist would take the majority of her clients with her—I didn't begrudge her that right or the clients that choice. However, the lack of business was not only bringing me down, but also making me worry a bit about income.

I had some money from Grandpa still, and I had a pretty decent little income coming in from some art I sold online. The projects I got contracted for paid pretty well, but taking on more of those left me less time for the shop.

Taking a deep breath, I pushed away the worries.

I was a damn good tattoo artist and my previous years of work were proof of that. I had an amazing portfolio. I was competitively priced. And the location of this shop was a potential goldmine.

I knew all this coming into being a shop owner.

I also knew getting word out about my work and pulling in my own customers would be a lesson in patience.

Grandpa and I had sat down with a plan when I told him I wanted to buy Cravin' Ink Designs. The few clients I'd brought with me from past locations would hopefully be good word-of-mouth. With a little more focus on my side gigs for a while, I could float for quite a bit before I got into trouble.

By then, I'd have a larger client base.

My goal for now was to keep a clean and safe shop, impress the folks who stopped in to check it out, and get awesome designs inked onto as much skin as possible. The more of that I could do, the better chance I had of making this whole business owner thing work.

Meanwhile, I also needed to worry about my junker car, the need to move out on my own, and a gray-eyed boy whose smile I couldn't erase from my mind.

Who knew adulting would be such a mind-fuck at times?

TWO

Leighton Anthony Cruise

WHAT IN THE actual fuck was I doing?

Had I learned nothing from my disastrous past?

How had I gotten myself all twisted up over a dark haired, dark eyed, stoic, highly inked guy who chewed toothpicks like candy and drank his coffee black?

I hurried into the top-floor living space I shared with several others at Cravenwood apartments.

Even after living here for a couple years, I couldn't help but laugh at the name Cravenwood. As a proud gay man, I found myself *always* cravin' wood, so me living in this area of Midtown was absolutely perfect.

Even without the sexual innuendo on the community name, Cravenwood was exactly the right fit for me.

My parents would have happily had me live at their house for the rest of my life. I did *not* have a rough coming-out story. My entire family—in addition to likely knowing I was gay before I did—was beyond supportive. I'm sure there were some distant relatives who maybe would have turned up their noses, but my immediate family was great.

Mom, Dad, my sister Aleigha, they all loved me no matter what.

We all went to my first Pride together when I was in seventh grade.

They constantly wanted me to come visit and bring any boy I might be dating.

Living with them wouldn't be a hardship.

But I'd opted to move out on my own a couple years ago. I'd found a great job at Cravin'-a-Cup a few months before leaving home, and lucked out to land a spot at Cravenwood Apartments a short time later.

Our little Cravenwood bubble of the world truly did have almost everything a person could need. A lot of people who lived in or around Cravenwood loved the fact they never really *had* to leave for necessities unless they wanted to.

The great thing about Cravenwood Apartments was the way the new-ish manager had set up the two buildings. Cravenwood Apartments Tower A was three floors and stretched the entire length of the westside block. Cravenwood Apartments Tower B was also three floors, stretched the entire length of the eastside block, and faced CAT A.

Julian Barrows was the apartment manager and he was in charge of both towers—okay, they weren't exactly *towers* but the name worked. However, he resided in CAT A and let his assistant manager, Chloe, run CAT B. When Julian had taken over, he'd designated a large portion of the third floor on both towers to being residencies for folks who were employed on Cravenwood Block.

So, I'd lucked out with one of the top-floor living spaces.

Now, I had to say, the set-up of the apartments that were reserved for Cravenwood Block employees was a bit strange—but living so close to where I worked allowed me to overlook the uniqueness.

There were three employee residencies—each with room for eight individuals—on each tower. Employees on Cravenwood Block *could* opt for other apartment spaces, but they'd definitely lose out on the perk of top-floor living.

The top-floor apartments in both towers had private access to the rooftop pool, dining area, sauna and jacuzzi, gym, and lounge area.

The living space of each employee residency was designed to have a living room, a kitchen, a laundry, four double-occupancy bedrooms which share two bathrooms, and an additional bathroom near the laundry room.

The bedrooms were the unique part.

Whoever designed the space must have thought that a lot of adults living on their own wouldn't want to share a room like kids in a dorm, so the bedrooms had one door that opened to a shared little foyer or lounge-ish area, and then each sleeping area had its own door. The sleeping area had room for a queen-sized bed, dresser, and desk. There was a built-in closet and each room shared a bathroom with the neighboring room through the lounge area.

Hypothetically, a couple could share one sleeping area,

but the living-space would get really crowded if there were sixteen people rather than just eight. Maybe a couple here and there would be okay.

I jumped when someone behind me cleared their throat, slamming me from my random thoughts about the apartment situation.

Okay, maybe not so random since I'd sprinted up here in hopes of chatting with Julian about the prospect of offering Jett a room.

Jett.

The object of my infatuation.

The straight man I needed to leave well-enough alone.

The dark haired, dark eyed, inked up beauty I couldn't help but be drawn to.

Don't you remember how messing with a straight guy worked out for you last time?

"You look lost in thought," Julian, my friend, roommate, and apartment manager said as I stared out the kitchen window.

I turned to face him, shoving my hair from my face. "Yeah, guess I am. I've got a double shift, so I need to get back down there."

"But?" Julian cocked a brow. He was a soft-spoken, gentle giant who always saw right through me. "What's up? Can I help?"

That was Julian for you, always wanting to help others.

He and his half-brother, Ollie, were two of my closest friends.

"I don't want to put you in a bad spot, but what would it take to move someone to the top of the waiting list for that last bedroom?" I gestured over my shoulder to my room.

Julian studied me a moment.

The room he shared would soon be occupied by an employee from the Cravenwood Health Center.

The room Ollie shared had already been spoken for— and by spoken for, I meant Ollie *begged*—by the sexy older guy who ran the Cravenwood Education Center where Ollie was the music director—that situation was a whole-ass story, but it wasn't really mine to tell.

And the open room already had a deposit from two best friends—the bartender from Cravenwood Tap and the doctor from the health center.

That left just the bedroom shared with me.

Jett needed a place—or he *wanted* a place. I wasn't sure what his *need* situation was.

I wanted a roommate.

Okay, that wasn't true.

I didn't care that the bedroom next to me was empty.

I really didn't want some asshole to move in.

But overall, it wasn't a big deal.

So, the truth was, I *wanted* Jett to move in.

Wanted him nearby.

Wanted him as a friend.

Honestly, I wanted a lot more than that, but I could respect the guy not being interested.

If you're being really honest, you know damn well there's some sort of interest there. It's in his eyes. Even if he doesn't recognize it or understand it, it's there. And you want to see where it could go.

I sighed.

Yeah, so maybe that was true.

But I'd had miserable luck with straight guys in the past.

Okay, it was *one* guy. But things had gotten really serious, really fast, and I'd believed him when he said he'd eventually be okay with being with me.

Obviously, it never happened and I was left heartbroken when I finally admitted he'd just been using me for sex and had no intention of being with me outside of where he kept his dirty little secrets.

And now you're wanting to get involved with Jett?

No, not *involved*.

Casual sex wasn't involved.

Do you really think it's smart to invite a straight guy to be your roommate when you already have a boulder-sized crush on him?

I shrugged away the doubt.

Sexuality was a very fluid beast.

I wasn't inviting Jett to live with me in hopes of *turning him gay*. Shit like that wasn't respectful or realistic.

But having him as a roommate and friend would be nice.

I didn't think he'd be an asshole to live with.

And if that tiny spark of interest I saw from time-to-time when I chatted with him wanted to take root and grow into something casual, I'd have no problem with that.

I wasn't interested in falling for a straight guy again.

I wasn't looking for a forever.

I was happy with my job.

I was happy with my living situation and friends.

Adding no-strings-attached casual sex to my life would be icing on the cake.

And dealing with the fall-out when the casual sex blows up in your face and you're left rooming with the guy?

Pushing the thought aside, I shrugged. I'd deal with that if and when it happened.

Pffitt...that's definitely when *it happens.*

Ignoring my head, I looked to Julian for an answer.

"Is he an employee on Cravenwood Block?" Julian asked.

I nodded. "Yeah, he's the one who took over Cravin' Ink Designs. Jett Nelson." A silent shiver zinged through me at the thought of the ink on Jett's arms and all the possibly secret places he had other designs.

Julian shrugged. "If you're requesting him as a roommate and he's an employee, he gets first dibs. The waiting list is full, but that's for the other apartments, doesn't count for the employee residencies."

"Perfect. Can I bring him around for a tour?"

"Sure. Can I ask why you're so keen to have him as a roommate?" Julian crossed his arms over his chest and leaned against the kitchen doorway.

Feeling completely put on the spot, my hackles rose slightly. "No real reason. Seems nice, needs a place, we have a space. Figure it's better the devil you know and all that shit..."

Julian cocked a brow. "And you know this devil well?"

"Well enough." I pushed a chunk of hair from my forehead. "Been chatting with him for a couple weeks. Don't get any red flags. He mentioned wanting to live in

Cravenwood and I told him I might have an opportunity for him."

Julian nodded. "Can I ask something as a friend and not as the apartment manager?"

Not waiting for my answer, which was going to be me blurting out I couldn't stay for questions because I had to get back to work, Julian continued.

"Do you think it's wise to invite a guy you barely know to live with you when you have a potentially unrequited crush on him?" His words were soft, his caring concern evident.

I snorted. "Oh, it's not *potentially* unrequited," I lamented. "He's straight, and for now, that's his story and he's sticking to it."

"And you think you can change that?" Julian asked, disagreement filling his handsome face.

Shaking my head, I ran my hand through my hair. "Not at all. I've learned from all that shit with Stephon." Julian and Ollie had heard much of the story of my drama with my last real relationship—and by real relationship, I meant it left me in a sobbing, heartbroken heap and I hadn't had anything even close to resembling a relationship in the last two years. "I like Jett, there's no secret there. But the only possible option for us getting together is if he's down for hooking up. I have no plans on trying to change him. I'm not interested in a relationship."

Julian narrowed his eyes. "So, you're going to invite him to room with you, offer him casual sex if he ever wants to explore hooking up with a gay man, and you don't think any of this will cause problems?"

"Look, I'm twenty-five. I'm not saying it's a great plan,

but the guy needs a place to stay and I'm fine with him being my roommate. Anything beyond that will play out the way it's meant to be." I headed toward the door just as Ollie popped out of his room.

"What's playing out the way it's meant to be?" he asked, eyeing me and his big brother.

"Our dear Leighton is thinking with his dick and setting himself up for a painful outcome by inviting the straight guy he has a crush on to room with him—and *if* anything develops between them, it will be casual hookup sex and nothing else," Julian deadpanned, filling his brother in and letting me know once again what he thought of the plan.

Ollie, reddish brown hair, dark brown eyes, scruffy red-haired jawline, eyed me as if waiting on me to say Julian had it wrong. When I just shrugged, Ollie chuckled. "Sounds like a terrible idea, count me in."

I grinned at my friend and laughed.

Julian groaned. "You two are trouble. You shouldn't be allowed together."

"Which is why you didn't let us room together," Ollie said. Turning his attention to me, he continued, "You won't believe Sebastian. Absolutely gorgeous, smart, serious, older, mmmm. The things I could do to that man."

I gave him a fist bump, but asked Julian, "So, you're okay with your brother possibly hooking up with his new roommate, but I can't do the same?"

"No," Julian answered, frowning. "I'm not *okay* with Ollie's hopes and dreams involving Sebastian Evans being his happily ever after, but there's a difference."

When Ollie and I both waited, Julian huffed and went on. "One, Sebastian is more mature and I doubt he'll allow himself to fall for Ollie's incessant flirting. Two, you already have a lot of painful baggage thanks to your past with a straight guy, I don't think it's smart to invite more trouble with Jett."

"I should only room with gay men?" I snapped. "I can't just be friends with a straight man?"

"No. I'm just saying I think rooming with a man you have a crush on is probably not the best plan." Julian held up his hands. "But I can see when I'm talking to a brick wall. You two do what you want, you're not going to listen to me anyway. Just know I'll be here when the heartbreak crashes down."

Ollie and I glanced at each other and grinned right before we both rushed Julian and wrapped our arms around him.

"Our gentle giant," I crooned.

"Always the caretaker," Ollie murmured into Julian's chest.

"Shut up, both of you," Julian muttered.

"What about the new guy moving in with you?" I asked with a waggle of my brows. "Shaw? I didn't see much of him, but he looked cute."

Julian snorted. "He's eleven years my junior. Not only do I have zero business messing with anyone that young, I'm smart enough to know getting involved with a roommate is a terrible idea."

"Well, when we're old and decrepit like you," Ollie said, rolling his eyes at Julian acting as if thirty-five was ancient, "maybe we'll have all your sage wisdom. Until then, I guess we just have to live our lives."

I nodded. "I'm here to be good to people and have fun."

"A good time, not a long time," Ollie crowed.

"Bumps in the road are bound to happen, but as long as the majority of my time is happy, I'm not gonna complain." I shrugged.

Julian sighed and shook his head. "Bring Jett to tour the place whenever. Have him contact me about setting up a meeting to sign paperwork if he wants the room."

The rest of the day flew by.

Work was great—I knew people thought I was wasting my time at Cravin'-a-Cup, but I truly *liked* working as a barista. I was good at what I did, never got bored, had health benefits, and made a decent enough living I could save *and* splurge from time-to-time. I had no desire to shove myself in a nine-to-five box and watch my life slowly slip away.

Sure, when I was older, maybe the job wouldn't be what I wanted. I had a degree in general studies and I could go back to school if and when I decided it was what I wanted to do.

For now, creating coffee art, providing scrumptious treats, and chatting with interesting people was all I needed.

About an hour before my shift ended, the bells over the door chimed. Even with my back turned to the door, I *knew* it was Jett. I wasn't sure how, but my body tingled and the atmosphere of the shop shifted.

He glanced around awkwardly, as if he'd never walked into a coffee shop.

Jett in his usual tight t-shirts stretched over his sexy, inked arms, and jeans that fit him like a damn glove was *hot*.

Jett in a tight t-shirt, joggers that curved his ass just right, and glasses I'd never seen him in? Well, that was just a damn walking wet dream.

The place was pretty full, but the counter was empty. I smiled and met Jett at the register. "Hey, sugar, what brings you in? Couldn't get your mind off me? Just had to see me one last time before heading home?" I leaned in and whispered, "Spank bank fodder? I get it, that's cool. Not everyone can handle being the object of a hot guy's sexual fantasies, but I'm totally down for it."

Jett studied me for a moment. "I'm always torn between trying to decide how serious you are with the shit that comes from your mouth and wondering what the hell is wrong with you. Do you talk like that to everyone?"

I smirked. "Nope. Just the hot guys I have absolutely no chance with." Winking, I moved the conversation to a more neutral topic. "What can I get you, baby doll?"

Jett rolled his dark eyes behind his glasses and shifted the toothpick to the corner of his mouth. "I'm done at the shop for the night. Thought I'd grab a coffee for the drive home. Just the house blend, please."

We were comfortably quiet during the payment portion and Jett moved down the counter to the pick-up spot.

"I like the glasses," I said, bringing him his coffee a couple moments later.

He ducked his head, pulling the toothpick out of his mouth and tossing it in the trashcan. "Thanks. There's a shower at the shop so I cleaned up before heading home. My contacts were dry after long appointments today, so I switched them out."

"You get to do some awesome designs today?" I asked, wanting desperately to keep him talking.

"Yeah, both turned out really good." He pulled out his phone and showed me his work.

"Those are amazing. I can't believe you don't have a waiting list for appointments. You're really good."

Jett snorted. "In my dreams." He shook his head and sipped his coffee. "No, for real though, I'd like to think that will be more a reality down the road. Right now, I just need to get more clients on the books. Word of mouth is a great thing, so the more folks I can get ink on, the better the chance I'll fill my chair enough to make a living."

"Well, count me in for a good inking in the future." Sexually suggestive comment? Don't mind if I do. "I'm saving up money. I want something on my ass cheek and something on my lower abdomen near my hip bone. I'll show anyone willing to look and tell them all about the fantastic artist who marked me." Okay, that was *supposed* to just be flirty and stupid, but the thought actually turned me on.

Jett laughed. "I'll give you a ten percent discount if you promise to tell all your friends." I'd heard the man laugh a couple times and each event made me realize it was a sound I wanted to hear from here to eternity.

"Deal." I reached out and nearly gasped when our

palms pressed together. The heat sizzled between us. How was this man not gay? At least bi or pan? Was the universe conspiring against me? "Oh! You still interested in that apartment?"

Jett's eyes went wide. "Yeah. I mean, rent will play a big factor, but definitely."

"Okay." I rubbed my hands together. "Any chance you can wait until I'm off and I'll tell you all about it?"

Jett gave a nod and sipped his coffee. "I'll be out back at the picnic tables."

While Jett exited to go to the picnic area of the playground behind the shop, I swept into action and did about an hour's worth of work in fifteen minutes. Flipping the sign to closed and chatting with the few straggling patrons who hadn't gotten the hint when I started cleaning, I lamented that my closing job had been half-assed, but the morning crew would just have to deal with it.

And since I was part of the morning crew, I'd kick my own ass later.

For the moment, it didn't matter because Jett Nelson was waiting to talk to me.

The straight guy who is only waiting to talk to you because he needs a place to stay? Keep it in your pants, man, before you embarrass yourself.

Supposedly straight.

I wasn't setting out to change Jett—things just didn't work that way—but I liked him.

As a friend.

Someone to talk to.

A comfortable roommate.

Would I be completely down for burning up the sheets?

Hell, yeah.

But that wasn't my main goal here.

I swear, it wasn't.

Flipping off the light switch, locking the front door, and hanging up my apron, I headed to the back room.

I grabbed my iced coffee and scurried out the door, immediately spotting Jett sitting on the picnic table. The playground wasn't designed for nighttime play, but the lights were bright enough we weren't sitting in complete darkness.

Joining Jett on the table, I sipped my drink and bumped his shoulder.

"Okay, let me fill you in on the apartment. We can work out a time for you to come see it if you're interested."

When Jett nodded, I went on.

"We're on the top floor and get access to the private rooftop pool, sauna, jacuzzi, lounge, gym equipment, all that jazz. There are four rooms. Each room has a shared foyer-ish type area and then private sleeping quarters. Fits a queen bed, dresser, desk, in addition to the built-in closet. You'd have to bring your own furniture, except the closet, obviously. Two rooms share one bathroom, the other two share the other bathroom. There's a half-bath next to the laundry room. The kitchen, dining, and living rooms are decent sized. If each sleeping area was accommodating *two* bodies, the place would be too tightly packed—even though, on paper, it *could*. But if most of the sleeping areas only have one person, the apartment feels completely comfortable."

Jett's brows rose. "Sounds amazing. Also sounds like there's no way I could afford rent there."

I pressed a finger to his lips, doing my best to ignore his look of curious surprise and the zing traveling through my body at the contact. "Shhhh, none of that negative talk. The employee rate is amazing. *Plus*, utilities are included. The only thing you'd have to pay is food, your own internet if you don't like what's provided, personal laundry supplies. Parking can get expensive—you got a car?"

"Are you shitting me? All that's covered?" Jett shook his head. "I *have* a car, but if I can live here, I'd likely leave it at my grandpa's place instead of paying to park it when I probably wouldn't need it often—plus, it's pretty much a piece of shit."

"Well, I'll leave it to you and Julian to discuss the rent particulars, but I promise it's a very doable amount. You wanna set up a time to see the place?"

"Sounds good. What's your schedule like?"

I bumped his shoulder again. "I work pretty much every day, but I'm off most Tuesdays. What about you?"

"I flex my hours based on what clients need for the most part, but I'm usually able to take Tuesdays off— never much business on a Tuesday. I'm off a lot of Sundays, too, unless a client requests a special appointment."

"Tomorrow is Sunday, are you free?" I tried to push away the excited fluttering in my belly.

Jett winced. "Helping Grandpa clear some brush out back. What shift do you work on Monday?"

"I close, so I'd be available until about four."

"My first appointment is at three. Could we meet at noon maybe? That gives us time to see the place and I could maybe talk to Julian?"

Sucking the straw between my lips, savoring the sweet coffee as Jett's eyes honed in on my mouth, I pretended to consider. "Make it eleven-thirty and we'll meet for lunch at the diner."

Jett's brows shot up. "Meet for lunch, huh? Is that the price of finding a decent apartment?"

He was damn adorable when he teased. Like his social skills were rusty and he needed oiled like the Tin Man. Kinda gruff and could come across snappy, but so damn cute.

"It is. We're friends now, get used to it." I stood and tossed my cup in the trash. "Hand me your phone."

Jett eyed me but handed over his phone.

I quickly added my number to his contacts and texted myself.

"You've got my number in case we need to adjust plans. Now, walk me home."

"Damn, anyone ever tell you you're bossy as fuck?" Jett drained his own cup and threw it in the trash.

"Buttercup, it's not so much that I'm bossy, I just know what I want. Let's go."

By the time we'd crossed Cravenwood Avenue and reached CAT A, I was about to float away on Cloud Nine. Whether this guy ever became something sexual to me or not—okay, he was already fulfilling my jerk-off sessions, but you knew what I meant, right?—I found I absolutely adored spending time with him.

Hell, who knew?

Maybe Jett and I were truly meant to just be friends and I'd be okay with that.

Either way, I knew for a fact that inviting him to room with me was the right thing to do.

And I was excited to see how things panned out.

THREE

Jett

"HEY, I'm Julian. Leighton said he was bringing you over." A friendly-looking man who appeared to be about thirty-five to my twenty-five, approached me in the front-desk area of Cravenwood Tower A as Leighton and I walked through the door. "Nice to meet you. I hope Leighton explained I needed to meet with you earlier due to a busted pipe I have to go oversee repairs on."

"Hi, nice to meet you. Jett Nelson. Yeah," I said while shaking Julian's hand, Leighton grinning like a damn loon, "heard you've got a mess to deal with. Thanks for being willing to meet with me."

"All part of the job." Julian smiled. "Leigh, we're going to talk rent in my office. We'll be out in a bit."

I immediately liked that Julian was able to separate his friendship with Leighton from his apartment manager side. I wasn't destitute, but I wasn't keen on Leighton—or anyone, really—sitting in while Julian and I talked credit reports, income, and all it would entail to get me into Cravenwood.

Get me into Cravenwood.

I snorted, doing my best to cover the noise with a cough as I followed Julian into his office.

Wouldn't Leighton just *love* to get me into cravin' wood?

And now he had me making puns about cravin' wood like a teenager.

A fairly quick and painless thirty minutes later, Julian shook my hand. "I'll get all the paperwork lined up, but everything looks good. Since you're already a business owner here on Cravenwood Block and a current resident requested you as a roommate, the process won't take long. As long as you like the place and decide you want it, plan on moving in within the next few days if that works for you."

"Sounds great, thanks." Surely, I'd like the place, right? The rent was well-within my budget and the perks were crazy. I'd have to be insane to turn down the apartment. I'd miss living with Grandpa—after seven years, the old man had grown on me...let's be honest, he was the only *real* family I had—but saving gas money, having the gym, pool, and utilities paid was a no-brainer.

Leighton beamed as we walked out of Julian's office. "Well? What did you think? Will the rent work? Wanna see the place?"

Julian shook my hand, hugged Leighton and told him to behave, and waved as he headed out the door to CAT B for the water pipe repair.

"Unless it turns out you want me to sleep in a closet, wash my face in a piss bucket, or eat from the floor, I can't imagine a scenario where I *wouldn't* want this apartment."

Leighton rushed toward the elevator. "There are only three floors—the building is wide not tall...and, yes, there's a definite innuendo in there about girth versus length, but I'm going to leave it alone. For now." He pushed the *Up* button as he snickered.

"This is you leaving it alone?" I rolled my eyes, my stupid head and traitorous dick suddenly giving a lot more thought to girth and length than I *ever* had in my entire life. What in the hell had this man done to me?

Leighton shrugged. "What? I didn't say I was *good* at it, just that I was doing it. Anyway, the stairs aren't too terrible, only three flights, but the elevator isn't one of those scary death traps that smells like pee either."

"Good to know," I deadpanned and followed through the sliding doors.

As we exited the elevator, I could tell Leighton was nervous. It was weird how I'd never really paid much attention to others around me—except my grandfather—but for some reason, Leighton struck something in me and I picked up on his moods, his movements, his nuances.

And he was scared I wouldn't like the place.

As if me not liking the apartment would mean I didn't like him.

And that couldn't have been farther from the truth.

I liked Leighton.

Fuck.

For some damn reason, I *liked* him.

Not the way he wanted me to, but the fact I even liked him meant he'd gotten under my skin.

Could *you like him the way he wants you to? Do you want to like him that way?*

I ignored the question and the low thrum of heat in my gut.

This was *not* a line of thinking my brain had ever taken.

Ever.

No reason to start now just because a guy was flirty with me.

Is it truly just because he's flirty? Or something more?

Ugh, I hated how fucked up my head was.

I wanted to see the apartment, make sure Leighton knew he didn't have to be worried about me not liking the place, and get down the street to my appointment.

Lunch with Leighton at the diner first.

Nearly popping a vessel, I took a deep, calming breath; I needed to center myself and stop hashing and rehashing the situation.

"All right, let's see this place." Why was I so concerned about making sure Leighton was comfortable? Seriously, the guy had gotten to me good.

He swung open the door and I stepped in behind him, accidentally plastering myself to his back when he didn't move into the room as far as I expected him to.

"Shit, sorry," I mumbled, stepping aside and swallowing thickly against the imprint of his body pressed against mine.

"Never gonna complain about a hot man pressed into me. I'm a Cravenwood boy, after all," Leighton quipped, a saucy smile on his pretty face.

Damn it, stop thinking about his pretty face.

"Welcome to our humble abode." Leighton swept his arm around the room. "You already met Julian. *This* is his brother, Ollie."

A guy about my age stepped forward with a smile and a firm handshake. Dark red hair and a light smattering of freckles made him seem slightly younger, but his dark eyes reminded me of Julian—kinda like Ollie was a mixture of youthful and mature.

"Hi, nice to meet you. So, you're here to see the room?" Ollie asked.

I nodded. "Yeah, sounds like a great place to live."

He nodded. "It really is great. I love not needing a car —if I *have* to, I'll Uber it or rent a car for a trip. The perks of top-floor living are soooo worth it. And so far, we've not had problems with any of our roommates."

I wasn't completely sure if he was being conversational or making sure I understood no shit would be tolerated.

"I'm not a big partier. Pretty much go to work, do my art, eat, and sleep. I'm not wild, don't have crazy friends— or actually, *any* friends—and I'm responsible. I like a clean place, putting things where they belong, that type of thing." Julian had basically been concerned about my financials. Leighton was just happy I was giving the place a chance. But Ollie seemed protective.

Of Leighton?

The place?

Their little group?

After studying me for a moment, Ollie gave me a genuine smile. "You're all right. If Leighton *and* Julian both vouch for you, no worries. Do your part and we're all good.

"So, there's just three of you right now?" I glanced around a really spacious living room, dining room, and kitchen area. The four doors off the main living area must have been the bedrooms.

"A while back, we had eight. In the last six months, we've had turnover based on folks leaving Cravenwood. We've got four guys moving in soon, but you're lucky number eight," Ollie explained.

I shook my head. "I'm sure everyone has their reasons, but damn, I just got to Cravenwood, I'd hate to think of having to leave it."

"I hear that," Ollie agreed. "A few got different jobs. One got pregnant, one got a new girlfriend and moved in with her on the other side of town." He held up a hand. "I promise, no one moved because we're bad roommates. Well, at least not Julian and me," he teased as he put Leighton in a headlock.

"Hey, I'm a good roommate!" He frowned and tried to fix his hair. "I mean, I think I am. Aleigha and I shared a room for a while."

"Any of Leighton's negative roommate qualities are made up for by his cheery disposition, cute ass, and ability to always show up with free coffee and treats when it's most needed." Ollie laughed at Leighton's outrage.

"Is that all I am to you? A cute ass and coffee cow?" Leighton folded his arms over his chest.

"No, not at all. You're so much more than that. Don't forget the cheery disposition."

Leighton softened. "Well, my ass *is* nice." He bit his lip, winked at me, and slapped his ass before heading toward one of the closed doors. "Come on, baby cakes, let me show you where the magic happens."

I followed him.

"Okay, that room right there," he gestured to a green door, "will soon have Lucas and Dean living in it. They're like best friends or something. I think one is a doctor over at the health center and one of them is a bartender." He swept his hand over a blue door. "This one is Ollie and his soon-to-be-roommate Sebastian—if everything goes like Ollie hopes it will." Leighton pretended to whisper. "Ollie is all hot and bothered by the much older Sebastian. They work together at the education center and had a wild start. Ollie is the music director and Sebastian runs the whole business. Ollie wants Sebastian to tune his fiddle, tickle his ivories, bang his drum…"

"Oh god, stop," Ollie called out and slammed his door in our faces.

Leighton snickered. "This room," he pointed to an orange door, "is Julian's. His roommate is Shaw, he works at the health center, and he'll be moving in soon."

We made it to the last door.

"So, the first two rooms share a bathroom and these two rooms share a bathroom, but the spaces are pretty decent so nothing has ever really felt cramped."

My heart caught in my throat.

In all the times I'd thought about *rooming* with Leighton, I'd been thinking about sharing an apartment, not sharing an actual room.

I cleared my throat.

This was fine.

Everything was fine.

It wasn't like I had to share a bed with the guy.

Does that idea really *even bother you?*

Leighton opened the purple door and motioned me inside.

We walked into a cute little foyer area, kinda lounge-ish, with a door to the far right—bathroom—and two multicolored doors facing us.

"This one on the left is mine. The one on the right," Leighton gestured, "is yours."

I opened the door.

I was home.

That was the weirdest feeling in the world, but that's what washed over me.

From Julian, to Ollie, to the apartment as a whole—and especially to Leighton and this room—every single piece of a puzzle I hadn't even known I was working on clicked into place and I knew this was the exact place at the exact time I was supposed to be.

For someone who'd never really had friends, never really belonged outside of my grandfather loving me, feeling that sense of belonging meant the world to me.

"This is absolutely perfect. I love it."

"Really?" Leighton beamed.

"Yeah, I'm in."

"Welcome home, snookums." Leighton opened his arms.

I froze.

"Come on, your new roommate is a hugger." His arms fell slightly and he cocked his head. "Unless hugs make you super uncomfortable?"

I had the chance right then. I could have told Leighton

hugs made me uncomfortable. In reality, I was fairly neutral about hugs simply because my parents weren't huggers and my grandpa hugged me all the time. Outside of those people, I didn't have a lot of experience with hugging or not hugging.

"Nah, it's cool," were the words I heard coming from my mouth as I stepped closer to my new roommate. The spark in Leighton's pretty gray eyes and the happiness in his smile suddenly seemed worth any and all hugs he ever wanted to give me.

With little time to prepare, I found myself with Leighton's arms wrapped around me and my own arms doing some awkward semblance of an embrace as he squealed, "I can't believe I basically got to pick my roommate. That almost never happens. You mostly just take a risk and hope you don't get an asshole."

Leighton stepped back, my body immediately—and very curiously—missing the heat of him against me.

"I mean, I guess you could still turn out to be an asshole, but at least you're pretty, gainfully employed, and can hook me up with killer ink," he continued to ramble. "Okay, let's get lunch before we have to go to work."

After a quick welcome handshake and friendly goodbye with Ollie, we headed down the stairs and around the corner to the diner.

"Hey," I said, before I could think through my words.

"Yeah?"

"You know I'm not gay, right? You still okay with me taking the room?"

Leighton stopped on the sidewalk and pulled me to a little window alcove. "Look, you don't have to worry about me. I'm a thousand percent gay, but I know you can't *turn* a person's sexuality." He waved his hand. "Now, we don't have time for my spiel on how sexuality is fluid and changes for a lot of people…that's more a late-night dish sesh with tubs of ice cream. I respect you and I'd never purposely put you into a situation where you feel pressured or uncomfortable—if I do it without knowing, please let me know…although, I *am* pretty outrageous most of the time, so I can't promise to change the real me."

I cocked my head. "But?" Leighton had taken my *I'm straight* statement a little too easily.

He popped a fist onto his hip and batted his lashes. "If you ever feel the fluid sexuality getting curious and need a safe spot to land when it comes to some casual experimentation, I'm your boy."

Pretty sure my eyes bugged out of my head.

"I have some ugly, beat-up, poop green baggage from the past I'd really rather not keep dragging around."

I scowled.

Leighton chuckled. "What I mean is that I'm not looking for anything real or serious. I'm all for a safe, sane, and consensual good time. I'll have that with or without my gorgeous new roommate—but on the chance that he decides he's curious, I just want him to know I'm down to play around, keep things casual, and make sure nothing gets weird."

Crossing my arms over my chest—knowing it made me look bigger and meaner, but secretly loving the fact Leighton never even blinked…kinda like he knew I'd never hurt him and I could be trusted no matter what—I stared down at him. "Let me get this straight..." I rolled my eyes at his snort of laughter. "You're not looking for love or anything *real*, but it feels like a good idea to offer no-strings-attached sex to your straight roommate, and you don't think this has the potential to be a disaster?"

Leighton bit his lip and stepped close enough his lower chest bumped into my arms. "I find it *very* interesting that you don't seem the least bit turned off by the fact I offered to slake your curiosities about sex with men."

I stared at him for a moment longer, shifted my toothpick from one side of my mouth to the other, shook my head, and huffed. "I'm beginning to think I need to worry about you."

"Oh, baby cakes, you most definitely need to worry about me. I'm going to end up being your best friend, your juiciest dream, and your worst nightmare all rolled into one." He turned toward the diner.

"I think that was supposed to be a threat, but you somehow make it sound like a good time," I mumbled, following him down the sidewalk.

"Damn right I do. Come on, I'm hungry."

We walked into the Cravenwood Diner and I was hit with yet another wave of how *right* things felt. Maybe the stress of owning my own business, planning a move to a new town, and meeting a handful of new people all in a short span of time was getting to me.

Or maybe you're just hitting your stride and coming into your own.

Yeah.

Maybe.

I bit back a smile and tossed my toothpick in the trash.

Coming into my own.

I liked that.

Lunch with Leighton turned out to be…interesting?

He was a friendly person and it quickly became evident he enjoyed chatting with people. No wonder he liked his job at the coffee shop.

"Hey, man, we never did end up making plans for that movie marathon," a guy said with a wink for Leighton after eyeing me up and down. "We should make it happen."

"Oh, um, yeah. Definitely. See, the thing is…" Leighton stumbled.

"Sorry, man. He's helping me move so he'll be busy for a while. Can he get a raincheck for when he's not so swamped?" I said, leaving no room for argument.

The guy frowned. "Yeah, sure. Hit me up when you're free."

Leighton sank into the booth when the guy was gone. "Thanks for that. I knew having you as a roommate was going to be great, but I didn't realize it would mean having my own built-in filtration system."

I snorted. "Filtration system?"

Leighton grinned. "Yeah. You just filtered out the riffraff and gave me a chance to conveniently forget that guy's number. The sex was decent, but he's like a cling-on who just doesn't take no for an answer."

I raised a brow and Leighton feigned a shocked gasp making us both laugh.

"Why not just tell him thanks but no thanks?" I asked.

"I don't know. I don't like upsetting people."

I nudged his foot under the table. "Gotta get past that. You don't go putting yourself in uncomfortable situations just because you're afraid to upset others. You stand up for yourself first and foremost. Always."

The pink hue to Leighton's cheeks, and the wide-eyed wonder in his gray eyes, did something to me. Nothing I could name, but something all the same.

Our food arrived and I learned quickly that Leighton was kinda a picky eater.

"Why not just ask for your sandwich with only cheese?" I asked as he picked off the lettuce, tomato, and onion.

"Doesn't hurt to pick it off and it's easier than asking for it without."

"And you'd rather not upset the fry cook by making him think you don't want his veggies?" I cocked a brow.

"Maybe?" Leighton blushed. "It's really no big deal."

I pointed a fry in his direction. "What if they run out of the veggie trimmings and someone who *wants* them can't have them? All while you're sitting over here wasting them because you don't want to put out the waitress or offend a fry cook?"

The look on Leighton's face said he'd never thought if it that way before.

"So, no lettuce, tomato, or onion. Besides cheese, what else would you want on it?"

He lifted a shoulder. "If it came with pickles, I'd eat them."

"Do you *want* pickles?"

Leighton bit his lip. "I like pickles," he muttered.

I huffed. "Your assignment the next time you order

food is to order it exactly the way you want it. No worries about others, just the way *you* want it."

He nibbled on the inside of his lip and nodded. "I can try that."

"Do you get upset when people place specific or needy orders at the shop?"

"Not at all," he said around a big bite of his sandwich, "I want to help make sure it's just the way they like it."

"Others are likely the same," I said. "Don't push away what you want out of fear of making someone mad. You have every right to have a sandwich just the way you want it."

"It's truly not a big deal to take it off," Leighton said. "But I'd never really thought about the fact I'm wasting it. I'll ask for it without next time."

"And add pickles," I said.

"And add pickles."

When he'd eaten his last fry, Leighton grabbed the dessert menu. "Will you split bread pudding with me? It's huge and I don't want the whole thing, but it's soooo good."

"Well, you found one of my weaknesses. I probably could have resisted almost anything else, but bread pudding is my favorite."

"Note to self, seduce Jett with bread pudding if I ever want a true chance."

I laughed and we ordered the dessert.

And I didn't even let myself think of what Leighton's seduction by bread pudding would entail.

Nope, wasn't even going to let my mind go there.

FOUR

Leighton
_____

"DUDE, YOU NEED TO CHILL OUT," Ollie said. "You've worn a path on the carpet."

"Sorry, just excited for him to get moved in."

Jett had brought a few things to the apartment over the last week, but his grandpa was helping him bring his bed and dresser.

"They should be here soon," I rambled. "I'm nervous about meeting his grandpa. And tonight will be the first night he sleeps in his room. What if he decides it's not for him?"

"Well, he'd be out a deposit and first month's rent, so I doubt he's going to split." Ollie slapped a hand on my shoulder. "For real, chill out. And stop making it seem like this guy is something special to you; I'm going to feel real bad for you when he gets a girlfriend and leaves your little gay heart pining away."

I huffed. "He *is* special. He's a friend. He's super close with his grandpa and I want the man to know his grandson is in a good place."

I chose to ignore the comment about a girlfriend because I already knew my fabulous heart would wither and die if I ever had to see Jett with a girl.

Prepare yourself, you damn little homo. You knew he was straight going into this. You knew friendship was the only thing you should ever actually hope for.

Every time my head tried to talk sense into me, my heart had a *yeah, but* ready.

Yeah, but...Jett opted to live here.

Opting to live somewhere is not a declaration of love.

Yeah, but...he's opening up to me. I'd consider him an actual friend even though we're kinda Odd Couple-ish.

Yeah, but...I swear I'm not making up the occasional glint of desire and curiosity in his eyes. True, maybe it's wishful thinking, but I know when a guy is interested, and Jett definitely checks me out.

So, do you wanna take that budding real *friendship and throw it away with a quick curiosity fuck?*

All I heard was *quick curiosity fuck.*

Yes. Yes, please. Where do I sign up?

A ruckus in the hallway pulled me from my thoughts.

Ollie swung open the door in time to see Julian and Jett maneuvering a dresser down the hallway. The pushcart seemed to be helping, but the large wooden piece had awkward written all over it.

Once they'd dropped the dresser off in Jett's room, they made their way back through the living room. I gave a little smile and wave, but Jett just grunted.

"We need to get the mattress and bed up here," he said in way of explanation for why they weren't stopping to talk.

"Day one and you already look like a kicked puppy," Ollie said. "Why do this shit to yourself?"

"Little too late for that," I snapped. Running a hand over my face, I sighed. "Sorry, don't mean to take it out on you. Overall, he's my friend and I want him to be happy here. I don't know why I'm so concerned about his grandpa liking me."

Ollie hugged me close to his side. "Because you always want everyone to like you. Which usually isn't a problem because everyone *does* like you."

"But when people like Stephon, and possibly Jett's grandpa, don't like me, I take it personally and get all butt-hurt."

Ollie snorted. "Well, I'm pretty sure your asshole ex who never had an iota of a plan to leave his girlfriend…"

"Whom I had no clue about until *well* into the relationship, I'd like to add."

"Noted. But I don't think Stephon was anything like Jett's grandpa. First, you're not fucking Grandpa."

I slapped a hand against his chest. "Stop, that's just wrong. I mean, I'm all for an age-gap, but that's too much."

Ollie snickered. "Second, Grandpa is just your friend's relative. You two don't have to be best buddies in order for you and Jett to be friends." He eyed me suspiciously. "Unless that damn little homo heart of yours has already gone and concocted a story around you and Jett meaning more to each other and Grandpa being all for it."

I was saved from answering—although, let's be real, Ollie knew me well enough to know the answer—by the mattress appearing through the door.

When the crew of three made their way down for the bed, I went with them, offering to grab everyone a coffee. I took orders and headed to Cravin'-a-Cup, feeling at least somewhat helpful.

Once we were all back in the apartment, I handed out two black coffees, one with cream, a mocha, and my own special mixture—which was less coffee, more extras.

"So, you must be Leighton," Grandpa Nelson said, sticking out his hand. "Thanks for the coffee."

"Hi, it's nice to meet you. No problem. It's a perk of working there." I felt myself spiraling into a ramble, so I sipped my drink to shut my own mouth.

"This is a great place you boys have here. I think Jett did a good job landing himself a room." Grandpa sipped his coffee.

"It's a good place to live. Walking distance to a lot of things, close enough to most everything else," Ollie said, maybe knowing it was best if I calmed myself before I started speaking much.

We visited for a bit, but Grandpa soon said it was time for him to head out.

"You've got those casseroles in the freezer. Those should last for a while. We'll cook up some more when they get low," Jett said, walking toward the door.

"Son, I've been taking care of myself for quite a while now. Gonna miss you, but I can handle myself. Plus, I've got neighbors; we check in on each other."

"Leighton, can you go with Jett and make sure this mail key works on your way back up?" Julian asked, tossing me the tiny key. Ollie gave him a look like he'd lost his mind, but Julian just shrugged. "I had a few new ones made, but I haven't had a chance to test them out. I forgot to show Jett where the boxes are."

Thrilled to have a reason to tag along with Jett and Grandpa, I shot Julian a grateful smile.

When we reached the lobby area, I gave Grandpa Nelson a hug. "We'll take good care of him, promise."

"I have no doubt. Glad I got to meet you all and put faces with names."

"You'll have to come back when all the roommates are moved in. We'll have a game night or something," I said, having no idea where the words came from, but knowing Jett would like to have his grandpa visit.

"You wanna test that key now?" Jett asked, his voice gruff.

"Nah, walk Grandpa out. I'll hang out in here until you're back."

Ten minutes later when Jett returned, I could tell by the set of his jaw he was upset.

"I like your grandpa," I offered. "Seems like a great guy to have on your side."

Jett chomped so hard on his toothpick I expected it to splinter into tiny shards. "Yeah, he's the best. He's the only reason I didn't go insane with my parents. I spent almost every weekend with him. When I turned eighteen, I moved in with him and never looked back."

"I meant what I said about him coming to visit. We could have a big nacho bar and cards. Maybe a board game? Dungeons and Dragons would be cool, but I'm not sure the entire crew would be down for that."

"He'd like to come visit, I'm sure. He's a social

butterfly. Always at a friend's house or inviting friends over. Loves to put on a pot of coffee and just shoot the shit." Jett tossed the toothpick and popped another one in his mouth.

"What's with the toothpicks? I mean, you never seem to be using them to actually clean chunks of meat from between your teeth," I said.

Jett snorted. "Lovely image. I quit smoking years ago, but found I missed having something in my mouth. Started gnawing on my nails which was disgusting, so I tried toothpicks. They kinda stuck."

"My new bedroom buddy has an oral fixation, good to know," I teased. Leaning in close as we walked toward the mailboxes, I fake whispered, "Just to let you know, I'm down to help *any* time you need something in your mouth."

Jett coughed so hard I thought he'd accidentally sucked the toothpick down his throat. "Damn it, don't say shit like that without a warning."

"Doll baby, I *am* a warning." I gestured up and down my body before doing a spin. "Befriend at your own risk."

"Can you really say *I* befriended *you*? Pretty sure you stalked me, ambushed me, wore me down, and forced me to be your friend."

I blinked.

"And? I'm not seeing your point."

Jett laughed and wrapped his arm around my neck, rubbing a fist against the top of my head. "You're not right. Also, don't tell people we're bedroom buddies."

"What? I thought it had a nice ring to it."

"No."

We checked to see the mail key worked—which I knew it would, Julian would have already tested it out. I think he just sent me with Jett as a distraction, knowing saying goodbye to Grandpa would be hard.

Later that night, I got home from a closing shift, kicked off my shoes at the door, and found Jett in the kitchen scrambling eggs. Dressed in a pair of loose-fitting lounge pants and nothing else, he was sex on legs.

From the feel and sounds of the apartment, Julian and Ollie were either out or holed-up in their rooms. The other newbies would be arriving within the next few days.

So, instead of retreating to my room to beat off to images of Jett without his shirt like any self-respecting gay man would do, I opted to torture myself by staying in the kitchen and working on our friendship.

"Hiya, sugar lips," I said, sidling up beside Jett. "Those smell delish. Can I have some?"

Jett huffed and bumped me with his hip. "Fine. But get me more eggs. Maybe make some toast? And I'm not your sugar lips."

"Mmmm, but you could be."

I handed him more eggs and set to work making the toast. "Get settled in okay?"

Jett grunted. "Yeah. The room is great. Gonna take me a while to not feel like I'm intruding in other people's spaces. Grandpa's house was pretty big and I'd been there so long I didn't really feel like a visitor."

"You're not a visitor here, either. You pay your rent the same as the rest of us. Julian told you about the way groceries work, right?"

"Yeah, if it's labeled, it's off limits. If no label, it's free use as long as you're sensible about it."

"Yep. And the bathrooms are pretty easy. Four guys sharing one bathroom isn't ideal, but as long as we keep our time in there to *just* using the restroom and showering —do our hair and whatnot in our rooms—it works out okay."

I buttered the toast as Jett piled two plates with eggs.

"Eating in the living room okay?" he asked.

"As long as you aren't a total slob about it," I teased.

Jett rolled his eyes at my comment—it had quickly become evident that Jett was super organized and neat.

"So, the others move in soon?" he asked around a bite of eggs as we halfway watched the late news.

"Yeah. I don't remember the exact schedule, but anywhere from a couple days to a week and the place should be full." I stretched out my leg and nudged his thigh with my foot. "Don't stress. I've lived here with all eight people, it's not too terrible. Ollie knows Sebastian so he can't be too bad. Julian said he felt good about Shaw. Dean and Lucas are the unknowns, but they're best friends—plus, how bad can a bartender and a doctor be?" I snorted. "That almost sounds like the beginning of a joke."

"It's cool. I'm grateful for the place. Already saved money not having to fill up my gas-guzzler. Just weird going from living with one person to living with seven."

"Just think, that's seven potential customers." I waggled my brows. "Or one guaranteed customer and six potentials. Even if your other roomies don't want to get under your gun—and yes, I *am* the queen of sexual innuendos poorly concealed as innocent remarks—they'll maybe have friends who want ink and they can be all like, 'Oh hey, my roommate is a tattoo artist. You should go check him out.'"

Jett stared at me for a moment before he huffed out a laugh and continued eating. "Do you sit around in your free time and write down flirty things you can say?"

"Oh no, that is one hundred percent on-the-fly natural talent, pumpkin."

"No."

"Cupcake?"

"No."

"You're no fun."

We finished up our late-night snack in comfortable silence.

That was just one of the things I liked about Jett. Even though he wasn't usually quite sure what to make of me, we had an easiness between us.

Was there sexual tension?

Well, duh. I mean, at least on my part.

And I swore Jett wasn't completely uninterested.

But beyond that, he had finally accepted me into his bubble.

Maybe I'd pushed and elbowed my way in—okay, I'd definitely taken a battering ram to the situation—but he didn't *have* to let me in. Jett wanted friends—whether he'd admit it or not...hell, whether he even realized it or not—and he needed a person like me who set his mind to something and didn't give up.

"You need the shower?" I asked, knowing damn well

I'd be taking at least two minutes longer under the steamy water as I rubbed one out to visions of Jett pushing me to my knees.

"Nah, I'm good. Just let me brush my teeth then it's all yours."

When Jett emerged from the bathroom, I was lounging on the little loveseat in our foyer area. "Ohhhh, I thought of something, roomie."

"Oh lord," Jett mumbled.

"Our beds share a wall. We should have a code. Like one knock is *hi*. Two knocks is *good night*. Three knocks is *you okay*? Or maybe *I love you*. Hmmm, could be *I want toast*. Or even *down to fuck*. Okay, so the knocking might be a little tricky without context past a couple taps."

Jett just shook his head. "I think we're good."

"Yeah, you're right. We'll just stick to one and two taps. We can keep three for *you okay*. Only switch to *I love you* if the heavens open up and rain the miracle of all miracles down on me."

He leaned against his doorway. "A miracle like you stop talking?"

I stood and stripped my shirt over my head, loving the instant color on Jett's cheeks and the way his eyes darted around the room, trying to land anywhere but on my chest. What? He was bare-chested, I could be too.

"Nope. You know my hopes and dreams," I said with a wink. "Oh, speaking of our beds sharing a wall, let's agree to be respectful if we have bed buddies over. Just moving the bed an inch will save me from a night of misery and pain."

Jett seemed to be analyzing my words before he scowled. "Don't plan on having bed buddies over here. Kinda don't like the thought of others in my bed."

Good. I don't like the thought of others in your bed either.

"Well, if I'm not getting any from my main man, I can't promise I won't have to take the edge off from time-to-time, but I'll be sure to give a courtesy inch before getting pounded."

Jett's scowl deepened. "Thanks. Appreciate it," he deadpanned.

"I'm a good person like that." I patted his chest as I walked by—which was like a starving man reaching out and touching cake on his way to eat stale bread—and winked. "Just think, *all* of this goodness could be yours. All you gotta do is say the word."

Jett grunted and shot to his room, the door closing somewhat forcefully behind him.

I smiled and started the shower, making sure both bathroom doors were closed and locked. After washing my hair and body, I popped the top on Jett's body wash and sniffed it as I stroked my cock. My ass clenched, aching to be filled, but for the time being, my fist and imagination would have to do.

Truly, I probably needed to just give up on the dream of Jett, pull up the app on my phone, and find some cock on legs to fuck me senseless in hopes of taking my mind off the man I couldn't have.

But clearly, I was a glutton for punishment because the thought of any other man touching me at that point in time was *not* a turn-on, so I jerked myself with my eyes closed and let the scent of Jett's soap fill my senses.

What would he taste like? What would those hands feel like gripping my hair as his cock slid down my throat? Would his kisses be soft and curious or demanding and hungry? What would my name sound like on his lips as he groaned and shot his load into my ass?

My balls drew up tight.

Would Jett ever just close his eyes and pretend I was someone else? A hole is a hole, right? My throbbing cock and greedy ass wanted him so badly, I was willing to be used—willing to let him forget who and what I was—if it meant getting him inside me.

Shit.

That was fucked up.

Be honest, you're willing to let him use you, but deep down, you know there's a sliver of hope he'd finally open his eyes and realize how good it is, how good you are, and how much he truly wants you.

Yeah, so?

With my eyes still screwed shut, I imagined straddling Jett's waist and sinking my tight hole down his long, thick shaft inch-by-inch as he stretched me open.

I came with a muffled whimper against the crook of my elbow, my hot load splattering onto the tile as I milked the last few drops from my spent dick.

I was so fucked.

Crawling into bed a few minutes later, I sighed and tried to wrap my head around the situation.

Overall, I was glad to have Jett as a roommate and friend.

I'd eventually have to just accept he wasn't into me.

Except, every so often that spark of something *in his eyes makes you think* maybe, just maybe *there's a chance.*

I huffed and tried to get comfortable.

Yeah, there *was* that little tidbit.

But I knew I wouldn't pine for him *forever*.

My head, heart, and dick would all finally get on the same page when it came to Jett. I'd move on—probably after a week of sobbing into my pillow when he got a girlfriend.

But until that day arrived, I was determined to make the most of my time with Jett. I'd flirt. I'd be a friend. I'd make sure he knew he was wanted and welcomed.

And if anything came from it—a stronger friendship, an ass-drilling of my dreams, you know, I was open to pretty much anything—then we'd all be better for it.

With a sleepy smile on my face, still blissed out from blowing my load in the shower, I gave a light tap on the wall.

Just one.

Hi.

No answer.

Maybe he was asleep.

I tapped again.

Jett tapped back.

Hi.

I grinned like a fool even though I could almost hear his irritation in that one little tap.

Three taps.

You okay?

My chest seized at the thought of *I love you* and I was

most definitely *down to fuck*, but keeping it neutral with *you okay* was for the best.

One quick tap back.

Was that *yes*?

Realizing I was making *way* too much of knocks on a wall—as I was wont to do in several aspects of my simple existence—I rapped my knuckles on the wall in a final message.

Good night.

Silence.

And then two taps back.

Good night.

I was dead.

I'd gone and fallen for Jett even when I knew it wasn't smart.

And now my poor wittle homo heart would slowly waste away and die a miserable, lonely death.

But you helped Jett. You gave him a friend and a place to live.

And all I got was a metaphorical friendship ring—which was basically just a perpetual boner and a sad, empty ass.

———

"Hello, bunny butt," I crooned as I waltzed into the shop a week later.

"No." Jett shot me a look as if to say *not in front of a client*.

But the pale, greenish woman was smiling and glancing between us.

"Butt bunny?" I offered.

"No."

I pouted and pulled up a stool just outside of his work area. "Why? We could be butt bunnies together. So cute." Jett and I had settled into a comfortable routine, an enjoyable friendship, and I had a crush the size of Cravenwood and beyond.

"Leighton, I'm trying to run a business," Jett growled around a toothpick. "I'm sure my *client* would appreciate a *professional* atmosphere. I'll see you at home. Or after your shift. Or whatever. Just not here."

"Oh no, I don't mind. Leighton can distract me," the woman said.

"Perfect. Hi, I'm Leighton." I saw Jett clench his jaw, but he wasn't going to contradict his client.

"Jackie."

"Love the color. Jett can be my butt bunny, you can be my bunny butt." I moved my stool closer. "I want some ink, but I haven't decided exactly what just yet. Is this your first?"

We spent the next hour chatting and I watched in fascination as Jett worked his magic. He was beyond talented.

Jett nearly fell off his chair when Jackie said, "You two are so cute together. Like the whole opposites attract thing."

"We're not together," he bit out.

"Sadly, my dreams of making him a butt bunny of my very own have yet to come true," I said, pretending to be distraught.

Jackie studied us and the look on her face told me maybe others saw the connection between Jett and me as well. "Well, dreams *do* come true."

I swooned.

Jett scowled.

Jackie just winked and we went back to our chit-chat.

When Jackie was all finished, I told her to stop by Cravin'-a-Cup and say hi sometime. She left beaming about her new ink.

And then I was alone with Jett.

"Hey, sweets."

Jett pinched the bridge of his nose. "Leighton, you can't just sashay your way in here whenever you feel like it. I have a professional reputation to uphold."

I placed a hand on Jett's arm. "I came in to say hi, recognized the girl was looking a little green, spouted some stupid nicknames—which, were super cute and you know it—and thought maybe a bit of distraction was needed. It worked."

Jett's dark gaze bore into me. "How do you do that? How are you this guy who doesn't want to put anyone out by asking to hold the onion, but you'll totally risk pissing me off? How are you always worried about people not liking you, yet you say and do some of the most outrageous things?"

I shrugged. "I'm a walking contradiction, it's part of my charm. Look, had I walked in and judged the situation differently, I likely would have just said *hey*, asked if you needed anything, and left. But she wasn't doing well, was she?"

Jett sighed. "No. She was jumpy and tense. She was focused on every line, holding her breath, and likely would have called it quits before much longer if you hadn't walked in."

I gave a little curtsy.

"But that doesn't mean every client would have welcomed you intruding like that."

"I know and I wouldn't intrude like that with everyone. I'm a good judge of character. Take you, for instance. You've wanted to kick me to the curb since day one, but there's just something connecting us. You don't *want* to claim me as a friend, but you can't seem to help it. I didn't want to risk that friendship-only would be enough of a tether, so I invoked the roommate situation as a backup plan. And now, voila, we're peas in a pod. You're the peanut butter to my jelly, the ketchup to my mustard, the ham to my cheese."

Jett rolled his eyes. "Are you off? I've got to clean up, but she was my last appointment."

"I am. I was thinking about cheese fries and a vanilla Coke. You wanna join me?"

I saw the decision war on Jett's dark features. The way he chewed the toothpick indicated he wanted to say no. But his eyes softened and he smirked, shaking his head as if he couldn't help himself. "Yeah, sounds good. I'm starving. You wanna wait for me?"

"Obviously. You're stuck here cleaning up. That makes you the perfect captive audience." I settled in to watch as Jett set to work sanitizing and organizing his station. "You think you'll ever bring in another artist to work with you?"

He paused and glanced around the shop. "Why? You rethinking your burning desire to get under my gun?" Jett had loosened up a lot in the last week and I'd started seeing bits and pieces of a sense of humor—dry as a dead leaf, but still there.

"Duckie, at no time in this century will I *ever* rethink getting under your gun. And I'm also still down to have you tattoo me." I winked and blew him a kiss.

"Duckie?" Jett cocked a brow.

"What? It just came to me. Kinda cute?"

"No."

"It's unique."

"No."

I sighed. "I shall continue the quest for the perfect pet name. But for real, is bringing in other employees something you want to do?"

Jett shook his head. "Pet names not necessary. And I want to get a piercer sooner rather than later—brings in good crossover clients. Tattoo customers see the piercing work and want something for themselves. Piercing people see the ink work and give in to the pull to get their own. But I'm nowhere near busy enough to need or want another artist at this point. Not against it, just not something this place is ready for just yet."

We existed in a comfortable silence for a moment while Jett continued to clean.

"You're one of the most organized people I've ever met," I said. "I thought maybe it was just a shop thing, but now that we're bedroom buddies, I can see it carries over."

Jett snorted. "Coming from a guy I'm pretty sure was

raised by trolls—and that's just assuming trolls are messy —I'd say you're definitely the most *un*organized person I've ever met. Guarantee your socks don't match right now—and not because you're trying to be hip like the cool kids with mismatched, but because you couldn't find a single pair of matches when getting ready for work. How you show up day in and day out looking fit for a magazine when your room is a replica of destruction from a natural disaster is beyond me."

I batted my lashes and pressed a hand to my chest. "Ready for a magazine? That's maybe the nicest thing anyone has ever said to me."

"Don't forget raised by trolls and equivalent to a natural disaster."

Standing up as Jett threw away his paper towels and gathered the trash bag, I waved off his statement. "I choose to focus on the positives. I'm positive I'm hungry and I'm positive you think I'm cute enough to be on a magazine cover. Come on, let's go."

Jett rolled his eyes.

"You think any about that ink you want?" he asked after locking the front door and heading toward the back with the trash bag.

"I don't want anything stupid, but the one on my ass I don't want to be super cute or special because very few people will see it."

Jett cocked a brow as he glanced down at me.

"I mean, I'm sure several will see it." I waggled my brows. "But I don't want it to be some amazing piece I want to show everyone. Contrary to my flirty disposition, I don't actually want to bare my ass for *all* to see. And as

I've learned from you, not everyone even *wants* to see my ass." I sniffed in mock sadness. "But like, I don't want *insert dick here* with an arrow because someday I may have kids and they may catch glimpses of my ass—I remember thinking my dad's ass was really hairy when I was little—" I shivered. "Anyway, I don't think that's a smart move for a tattoo."

Jett cleared his throat. "Yeah, I definitely wouldn't be responsible for inking that on your ass. I'm down to ink you, but not with something like that."

I studied him as we walked. He was taller than my five-foot-eight by about three inches, but his broader build made him seem a lot bigger. "Would you put it on anyone else, just not me?" I wasn't sure which way I wanted him to answer.

Jett shrugged as we neared the diner. "Depends I guess. Definitely wouldn't ever do an *insert dick here* ass tattoo on a friend. Probably wouldn't on anyone else either, unless they were just a huge asshole and I figured getting a tattoo like that was karma for their treatment of others. And they'd have to sign off on it so I couldn't be held responsible."

"So, I'm a friend?" I smiled up at him.

He chuckled and rolled his eyes, throwing his arm around my neck and jostling me against his side. "Yes, Leighton. You're a friend. You won. You wore me down."

I knew we were joking around—and I knew friendship was all I should let myself hope for—but knowing he'd finally accepted me filled my heart with gooeyness.

And gives you hope for something more. Be honest. If you wore him down to friendship so easily, would moving beyond that really be all that difficult?

I pushed the thought from my head. I wasn't going to worry about that. I had Jett as a friend for now. There was no need to push for more. I was willing to let things happen. If we were meant to be, nature would take its course.

FIVE

Jett
_____

I WAS BEYOND FUCKED.

I'd been rooming with Leighton and the rest of the guys at Cravenwood for about a month.

Side note: The new guys were cool.

Shaw was quiet and I had a guess he had some sort of trauma in his past. He worked at the Cravenwood health center, was friends with Dean because they worked together, and Julian seemed to have adopted the position of *protector* the moment Shaw moved in.

Dean was a doctor at the health center. Seemed like a good guy.

Lucas was a bartender at Cravenwood Tap. He and Dean had been best friends since birth or something like that.

Sebastian was a former teacher and the director at the Cravenwood education center where Ollie taught music. He had the whole hot professor thing going on and he was the oldest of the eight of us, with Julian's thirty-five coming in second to Sebastian's forty-two.

Ollie panted after Sebastian like a dog begging for bacon. Sebastian pretended not to notice or care.

Shaw and Julian couldn't keep their eyes off each other. Julian swore the age difference and roommates thing would just be asking for trouble. I had a feeling he'd be asking for trouble before too long.

Dean and Lucas appeared to be a couple in every aspect of the word, but they swore they were just friends.

And that left Leighton and me.

A month ago, I would have said there was no *Leighton and me*.

But Leighton had definitely grown on me—wormed his way into my heart and under my skin—in a way that had me questioning…well, *everything*.

Between the time we spent together when he popped into the shop, the movies and video games at home, the texting back and forth and his stupid knocks on my bedroom wall, and the casual meals we grabbed together when our schedules matched up, Leighton and I spent *a lot* of time together.

And I loved every second of it.

I'd *never* spent as much time with anyone as I did with Leighton.

Not girlfriends, not even my grandpa, definitely not my parents, and not friends—and that was mostly because I didn't have anyone aside from Grandpa I'd consider a *friend*.

Until Leighton.

I mean, I actually had an apartment full of *friends* now. I didn't know all the guys super well, but we got along and I had a feeling they'd all help each other out if push came to shove.

Julian and Ollie were the two I was closest to, likely just because I'd known them longer. But Leighton had somehow become the person I thought of first when I had something good happen. Or something bad. Or something funny.

Fuck.

I wasn't sure what it all meant and I wasn't sure how to handle it.

Before Leighton blew into my life like the little hurricane he was, I would have said I was heterosexual with an unlucky history when it came to dating.

After Leighton sashayed his way into my life with his pretty, floppy blond hair, mesmerizing gray eyes, infectious smile, and insane sense of humor all rolled into a flirty ball of fabulousness, I couldn't stop myself from wondering if maybe my lackluster dating history had nothing to do with bad luck and everything to do with the fact I was dating the wrong people.

And by *wrong people* I meant...well, that was the part that got the most confusing.

When I tried to imagine replacing the *girls* I dated with *guys*, I felt nothing. No sense of regret or rightness.

When I replaced the girls I dated with Leighton?

Everything clicked in my head and my heart.

But that was insane, right?

I was twenty-five. Could I *just now* be realizing I was... what? Bisexual? Pansexual? Was there a word for falling hard for one specific person of the same gender? Or no matter the gender?

I'd heard people claim someone was *their person* and it never made any sense to me.

Until Leighton.

No explanation made as much sense as the words *Leighton is my person.*

And what the fuck was I supposed to do with these realizations? Leighton had made it clear he was into me. Was I supposed to tell him I *thought* I might be into him and just let it play out? What if I realized later I wasn't *as* into him as I thought? Or I wasn't into him the same way as he was into me?

Or...my stomach plummeted...I told him I was into him and he reminded me he was just on the lookout for sex, nothing *real* or long-term?

If the idea of *me* getting involved with someone else turned my stomach, the idea of *Leighton* being involved with someone else—whether just a random, meaningless hookup or a future, long-term relationship—nearly sent me to my knees.

Speaking of *to my knees*, I had absolutely no idea what I wanted with Leighton, I just *wanted* him. Wanted him by my side, talking to me, chilling with me, making me laugh, laughing at me...but I also wanted him physically, even if my head couldn't quite wrap around the logistics.

I didn't know a thing about homosexual sexual relationships. Okay, I mean, I got the gist of it, but I had no experience and no background knowledge.

I knew I'd never really been into giving oral sex, but receiving had generally been at least somewhat enjoyable. Would giving Leighton oral be any different? The way my cock perked up at the thought of anything involving Leighton's body, I had to think *yes*.

Beyond hand jobs and blowjobs, I didn't have enough information to form fantasies involving Leighton.

And was it even fair to think of him that way?

Maybe I needed to do some research?

Maybe I needed to...I didn't like the word *experiment* when it came to Leighton...but I also didn't want to do anything sexual with anyone *but* him...*fuck*, my head was beyond messed up.

"You seem deep in thought over there," Julian said quietly as he and Ollie returned from a trip to the grocery store. "You okay?"

Pushing away from the kitchen sink where I'd been staring out the window for the last twenty minutes, I grabbed two bags from Ollie. "Can I ask you guys some questions without it turning into some huge thing?" I blurted.

Julian cocked his head and Ollie smirked.

"We're friends," Ollie said. "You can ask us anything. The only way it would turn into some huge thing is if we thought you or another friend was in danger."

I glanced at my phone. Leighton wasn't due home for a while and the other guys were either at work or out.

"When did you know you weren't straight?" I asked, deciding to just bite the bullet.

Ollie's wide eyes sparkled.

Julian smiled.

Neither seemed completely surprised by my question —*that* was something I'd give some thought to later.

"Well," Julian began as he put two gallons of milk in

the fridge. "I didn't realize I was gay until my late twenties."

"Really?" I asked, somewhat surprised.

"Really. I thought I had shit luck with girls. Thought I was maybe asexual—even though I wanted sex. Then I fell hard for a guy at work—never ended up doing anything about it—and from that point on, I realized the shitty history with failed relationships with girls was because I was attracted to guys. I'd been a late bloomer as far as puberty, so it kinda made sense I figured out my sexuality later than some." Julian spoke in his usual quiet way as he emptied bags.

"And that's completely okay," Ollie added. "I think, as a whole, we're learning more and more that our identities can be very fluid. Obviously, some people are more static in their gender and sexuality—we wouldn't have a spectrum without fixed points—but a lot of people... especially these days as it's become more and more recognized and accepted thanks to generations before us...are realizing their gender or sexuality, or both, are fluid on that spectrum."

I let his words play through my head.

I'd *heard* people talk about sexuality and gender identity being fluid for some people, but I'd never thought it applied to *me*.

"For myself, I knew there was something different about me at a pretty young age." Ollie frowned. "Honestly, I can't wait until a day when cis gender and heterosexuality is no longer the default. When a kid doesn't have to feel *different* just because of who they're attracted to or the gender they identify with." He shook his head. "Anyway, I recognized pretty young that I loved girls as friends, but I wanted to look at boys, hang out with boys, dream about kissing boys."

We finished putting away groceries in a comfortable silence.

"You got a reason for asking?" Ollie asked.

I scowled. "Yes? No?" I huffed. "Maybe?"

"You can tell us if you want," Julian said. "We're not going to judge."

"What if I told you I'd recently realized I had feelings for someone of the same sex...not *all* people of the same sex, not even *some* people of the same sex, just *one* person of the same sex...what advice would you give me? Does that need a label? *Is* there even a label for that? Does it mean anything? If yes, *what* does it mean?"

Julian cocked his head and placed a hand on my shoulder. "I'd say it only needs a label if *you* feel like it needs one. And what it means is that you find yourself attracted to this person—just that. It doesn't have to be some huge meaning unless you want it to be."

"Do you think this person feels the same?" Ollie asked, crossing his arms across his chest.

I snorted. "Pretty sure we all know he does, but I'm also one hundred percent sure I can't be responsible for hurting him as I figure myself out."

Ollie gritted his teeth. "He's dealt with some real shit in his past, tread carefully or I swear to god I'll..."

Julian shot a warning glance at his brother and Ollie raised his hands in surrender as he backed out of the room. "Just don't hurt him."

I sighed as I watched Ollie retreat. "See, that's my

problem. I want to figure myself out. I want to know if these feelings could go somewhere—maybe *this* is why I've never had any kind of connection in the past—but I don't want to *use* him to figure my shit out."

Julian nodded. "Yeah, I hear ya. And Ollie is right, you do need to tread carefully. While I don't think you'd ever purposely hurt Leighton, I think the best option is honesty. Talk to him. Let him know how you're feeling. He's a big boy, he can make his own decisions. But you have to lay it all out for him—don't let him go into something without all the same information you have."

I nodded. "That makes sense. The last thing I want to do is hurt him, but I'm so confused by these feelings. Part of me thinks I should bury them and just continue being friends. Maybe that's the safest option."

Julian studied me for a moment. "Maybe, maybe not. I think the best option is approaching a friend with honesty and working things out between you that way. No others involved. No labels required. No societal stipulations. Just you and Leighton, heart-to-heart honesty, and the willingness to cooperate and take chances for each other."

My heart fluttered like a hummingbird attempting to fly out of my chest. "And if all of this puts our friendship on the line?"

Julian pursed his lips. "Your friendship is very new, but it's real. Anyone around you for more than five minutes can see that. I don't think true friendships are threatened by honesty. The bigger threat would be hiding your feelings, at least in my opinion."

"Thanks for being willing to listen and giving me more

shit to think about," I joked, slapping Julian on the back. "For real, I appreciate it."

An hour later, when Leighton breezed through the door, I was no closer to knowing how to approach him about my new feelings than I was that morning when I'd watched his cute ass leave for work. And acknowledging I thought his ass was cute was a bit overwhelming—but I also wanted to tell him, show him, act on the new feelings.

Although, 'new feelings' was a bit of a misnomer. In a way, my feelings were *very* new. I'd only known Leighton for a couple months—in the grand scheme of things, that wasn't long at all. On the other hand, I'd gotten tiny sparks of whatever was now growing and flaming to life between us since the first day he walked into my shop. Whether friendship or something more, we'd had a connection from the very beginning, even if it took my socially-stunted ass a bit longer to figure it out.

But having *any* feelings—especially for a guy—was new to me. I wanted to share it with my friend, but the fact my feelings were *for* my friend complicated things tremendously.

"Hey, daddy," Leighton quipped.

"Definitely not," I answered automatically. I'd gotten used to his constant ridiculous nicknames, but *daddy* didn't do it for me at all.

"Daddo?"

"No."

"Baby? Babe? My heart?"

I sighed. "Maybe we just give it a rest on the nicknames and let it come naturally?"

Leighton's gaze jerked to mine so fast I feared he'd hurt himself. "Ummm, that's new..." he hedged.

I shrugged. "Just sayin', don't try so hard." I should have said more. Right then and there, I should have just let him know I was questioning my entire existence. Instead, I took the easy way out. "How was work?"

Leighton launched into a story about a tired mom and her two rambunctious but adorable kids.

I sighed, loving his stories from work. I loved just leaning against the counter as he made himself a bowl of cereal while he spoke animatedly about his day.

"Oh! I've decided what I want on my ass. It's this cute little elephant." He opened a photo on his phone. "Would this be doable?"

I had absolutely no idea how in the hell I was going to get up close and personal with Leighton's ass and not come in my pants—and wasn't that just a fucked-up turn of events—but I wasn't sure how to tell him that. I cleared my throat. "Yeah, that's totally doable. Quick and easy."

Ollie piped up from the living room, "Let me see. I'll look at it on your ass if you want me to, but I want to see it now to know how much better Jett designs it."

Leighton scurried to the living room to show Ollie as Julian came through the door. After he'd seen the elephant Leighton wanted inked on his ass, Julian made his own bowl of cereal.

Soon, Shaw joined us and the five of us ended up sitting at the table, munching on late-night bowls of cereal.

"Jett, you'll be happy to know," Leighton said around a

big mouthful of cereal, "I'm encouraging my sad little homo heart to move on from you."

Pretty sure milk dribbled from my mouth when my entire body froze at his words.

"I'm stubborn and I'm not giving up hope completely, but a guy asked me out at work today. I don't think it's a love match, but he's cute and a bitch gets tired of his right hand sometimes." Leighton smiled and shrugged. "We definitely won't be picking out china patterns, but I'll hopefully be walking a bit funny for at least a day if I have anything to say about it."

I died.

Right there.

I was completely dead.

Julian's eyes bore into me.

Ollie popped up from the couch.

Leighton and Shaw were oblivious and kept right on eating.

But I was dead.

How did I respond to that?

Tell him to cancel his date because I'd recently realized I was attracted to him and *maybe* wanted to take things further even though I wasn't completely sure and had absolutely no idea what the hell I was doing?

Oh, and throw in I was pretty sure I not only wanted to fuck around with him and learn all about the joys of gay sex—would it be gay sex? Or just Jett and Leighton sex?

Fuck.

Right, tell him I wanted to learn about sex with him, but I also thought I maybe wanted *more* with him, but my head was all screwed up and I wasn't sure if all of these feelings would stick around and I didn't want to hurt him even though I desperately wanted to be with him in every sense of the word and everything I'd ever believed about myself had flown out the window the day I met him.

Yeah.

That would likely work out well.

Super.

Great.

I gave a quick shake of my head to Julian and Ollie.

They frowned, but I couldn't say anything right then.

Leighton wasn't going off to marry this guy.

It was just a date.

Hell, maybe in the time between now and the date, I'd realize my feelings weren't as strong as I thought they were—despite the fact my heart seriously felt as if it were breaking in two at that moment.

Leighton could go on his date.

His booty call.

Whatever you want to call it.

I'd get my head on straight—haha, straight. Yeah, if only my head was on *straight*, this confusing shit wouldn't be happening.

But in reality, I didn't want to go back to a time when I didn't know Leighton. He'd burst into my life and brought sunshine and smiles.

Sure, I was still a somewhat dark, stoic, tattooed guy people often assumed was an asshole, but Leighton had brought the real me out of that a bit.

And Leighton deserved a date with someone who at least had an inkling of who he was deep down within himself. I wasn't that person right then.

If you told Leighton the truth right now, he'd cancel his date and drop everything to help you figure things out. You know he would.

I did know that.

But asking Leighton to cancel a casual date just to help me figure out...what? What was I even trying to figure out?

A label?

Did I even need one?

Did I want one?

I liked Leighton.

I wanted to be with him.

Romantically.

Sexually.

And that scared the shit out of me.

Yeah, sure. Please cancel your date so I can fumble around with these new feelings I have for you and maybe, possibly, provide you with the worst sex of your life.

"That's great," I said as I finished off the last bit of milk in my bowl. "I'm beat, gonna head to bed."

"Jett, didn't you want to..." Ollie started.

"No, it's all good. Best to hold off for now. Not gonna hurt to wait."

Oh, it was gonna hurt all right.

Like a dagger to my heart.

But Leighton could go on his date, get laid, whatever, and that would give me some time to figure shit out.

Figure what shit out?

Did I truly like Leighton or was this just some sort of weird crush?

Is that even really a question?

Okay, liking Leighton wasn't questionable. I definitely liked him and wanted him around.

Did I want more with him? More than just friendship?

Maybe I just liked having a friend like Leighton all to myself after so many years of being a loner.

That answer would make a lot of sense...

But?

But you also have all these images in your head of holding his hand, kissing him, and crazy, sexy fantasies of sex with him. Things like that seem like more than just friendship type vibes.

I sighed.

Yeah, still a lot to figure out.

Is there, though? You know what you want and how you feel. Take Julian's advice and be honest with Leighton.

Leighton may not want what I think I'm wanting.

Sex? Leighton definitely wants sex.

No, the *more* part. I want sex, but I also want the friendship we already have plus something real—more long-term. And he's made it clear he's not looking for that after whatever happened in his past.

Be honest with him and let him decide what he does and doesn't want.

But what if I'm honest with what I want and it doesn't match up with what he wants? Then one or both of us ends up hurt.

Fuck.

Being a loner who sucked at dating—who never really moved beyond somewhat decent sex with girls who would never become anything more—was maybe lonely, but damn, at least it was somewhat easier on the emotions and my psyche.

I'd never understood when people said they *clicked* with someone or *it was love at first sight*. And honestly, neither of those were exactly what happened with Leighton. Yes, our friendship happened pretty quickly in the grand scheme of things, but the feelings growing in my chest had taken longer. Like we clicked right off, but I'd been oblivious.

You know how in supernatural type stories, the characters imprint or bond or some shit like that? Like there's very little explanation or understanding, just *boom*, yep, that's the one I'm meant to be with.

That's what it felt like with Leighton. Yeah, it had taken me longer to recognize it, but the time didn't change what I felt toward him.

Tell. Him. That.

Was it fair of me to drop some huge bomb on him when I wasn't even sure I understood all the shit going on in my head and heart? Interrupt his life with my self-realizations?

When it involves him, yes.

I showered and crawled into bed. Maybe when I had a better grasp on my feelings and the changes taking place within me, I'd be better able to approach Leighton with useful information rather than just a verbal and emotional upchuck that made very little sense.

What if Leighton goes on this date and starts something up with this guy?

My heart hurt.

If Leighton was happy, I had to be happy for him.

But if he's feeling some of what you're feeling, do you really think he could be happy with this other guy?

I heard the shower start and let myself imagine Leighton under the hot stream of water. The creamy paleness of his skin, the lean muscles of his abdomen and arms, the soft curves of his shoulders, ass, and waist.

Gripping my cock, I stroked slowly as I pictured him.

Naked.

Marked with my ink.

Wrapped in my arms.

Lips around my dick.

Fuck.

My cock leaked as I stroked.

My balls drew up tight.

With an image of my hips thrusting against him, our hard, leaking cocks rubbing together, I swallowed down a grunt of pleasure and shot my load all over my stomach.

When I finally came down from my high, the shower was off.

I wiped myself up with a shirt from my laundry basket and tucked it to the bottom so as not to accidentally grab it for anything later. Definitely needed to do a load of laundry soon.

As I settled into bed, thinking about Leighton—because that seemed to be *all* I did lately—I smiled to myself when I heard him.

Tap, tap, tap. You okay?

A warmth swelled in my chest as I thought about a possible day when *tap, tap, tap* could mean more.

I rapped my knuckles against the wall.

Tap. Yes.

Leighton returned a quick *tap, tap.*

Good night.

Tap, tap.

Good night.

What would it be like to have him in my bed, wrapped in my arms, whispering sweet words, and feathering kisses over his pretty lips?

I wanted that.

Wanted that like nothing I'd ever wanted before and it was confusing as hell, but I wanted him to know.

The desire I had to hold Leighton, to spend time with him, to take next steps with him was stronger than anything I'd ever felt for a combined twenty people in my past.

I was going to tell him.

Not that night.

Not the next day.

But I had to tell him.

He was at the center of this mess—not blaming him, just acknowledging that, without him, I wouldn't be in the situation—he needed to know.

Maybe I'd get his tattoo done first.

Let him go on his date first.

Then tell him.

SIX

Leighton

THE VERY LAST thing I wanted to do was go on a date with some guy who definitely wasn't the object of my affection.

However, I knew I needed to move on.

And quite honestly, a sliver of hope stuck in my heart that maybe, just *maybe*, Jett would see me going on a date and get jealous.

I *swore* there was something between us.

He could claim to be straight—and I didn't mean that in a way that indicated I thought all straight guys were secretly gay, just that something about Jett poked and prodded in the back of my mind and wouldn't let the hope die.

And let's face it, the default the world over is *straight* and we're so damn indoctrinated to all things heteronormative, it makes sense for people to assume they're straight until something or someone comes along and wakes them up to other possibilities—but I knew a spark of attraction when I saw one.

The other night when he didn't automatically tell me to stop with the nicknames, just to let something come naturally, I'd almost keeled over. Was that Jett's stoic way of letting me know he wasn't against me having a nickname for him, just not to push it too hard?

Maybe the same was true for whatever was possibly taking root and growing—ever so slowly—between us. Don't push it, just let it happen naturally.

So, I'd continue being *me* with Jett.

I'd go on my date because it was a decent distraction.

Maybe I'd get laid and ease the horniness.

Do you really think you'll be able to fuck some random date when your head and heart are so wrapped up in Jett?

Well, Jett's head and heart weren't wrapped up in me, so until we were an item, I could at least appease my greedy ass.

Riiiight. You're a total sap—a romantic at heart—if you expect anyone to believe you'll be able to fuck around with some guy when you're pining over Jett, you're ridiculous.

What? I couldn't help the fact that everything about Jett felt different. From the way we'd started out as friends to the way I sometimes caught him looking at me…all the way to how I'd known early on that I wanted something more than a fuck buddy with Jett.

He was the real thing in my heart.

And that poor organ was going to be crushed if I ever actually had to accept Jett and I had no future.

But I could go on a date.

Right?

Sure I could.

I could spend all night comparing the poor guy to Jett.

Get caught up thinking of Jett if and when I got naked with my date.

Shit.

I was a damn hot mess.

———

"YOU READY FOR THIS ASS, baby boo?" I asked Jett as I walked into the shop on tattoo day. "Because this ass is sooo ready for your gun."

Jett snorted and shook his head. "Let's get this party started," he teased.

He'd shown me his rendering of the elephant I wanted on my ass. I loved how he'd taken the example I'd shown him and made it all his own. I also loved that when he was explaining the changes he'd made, he had all of these reasons why his design fit me better.

Jett may have been *just* a friend—whether *for now* or *forever*—but he got me in a way a lot of friends never really did. He got me, he accepted me just the way I was—never trying to change me—and we balanced each other out perfectly. We were definitely the definition of the odd couple, but we made it work. And we made it work almost effortlessly.

Once he had his station all set up, he had me straddle the chair in just my boxers. "Not *exactly* my fantasy come to life, but I'm nearly naked, straddling your chair, and getting ready to show you my ass. I'll take it. For now. Baby steps."

Jett cleared his throat and chose to ignore my comment.

He knew it was often best to ignore a lot of my comments. "I usually let clients keep shorts on if that's what they're comfortable with, but it's easier if they get to underwear only or even nothing—less bulky cloth to work around. Show me again the area you want this placed," he said.

I pushed the edge of my boxers down—I'd opted for the loose-fitting boxers that day in the interest of making the tattoo easier—and slapped the far upper right side of my ass cheek. "Right here. As long as you think that area is a good spot."

"Yeah, it works fine right there." Jett set to work tucking towels under my shirt and into my boxers, explaining he did that to keep ink and any other fluids off my clothing.

Next, he went about cleaning and shaving the area while I pretended to be offended.

"My ass does *not* need to be shaved," I exclaimed, doing my best to push down the kinky flame burning in me at the thought of Jett shaving me.

"I shave the area for everyone. Your ass is fine." Jett cleared his throat. "I've seen some *really* hairy butts, you're all good."

I bit my lip and whimpered, really playing it up. "Damn, baby boo, I love when you tell me how fine my ass is."

Jett knocked over the bottle of alcohol he was reaching for.

Interesting.

"I'm going to put this outline on and have you approve the location. We can always move it if you don't like the position," Jett explained as his big warm hand smoothed over the transfer paper stuck to my ass.

A shiver of pleasure traveled through me as he rubbed his hand over the paper several more times before slowly peeling it away from my skin. It was a damn good thing I was straddling the chair because getting a boner for your tattoo artist as he prepped your ass for ink seemed a bit awkward.

"Okay, how's this?" Jett held up a mirror and spun my chair so I could see the reflection of my reflection and the adorable elephant outline on my ass.

"Exactly perfect. I can't wait to see it all done with the bright colors we planned. Let's goooooo." I tucked my arms under my head and settled in.

Jett spun me back around, locked the chair in place, and lowered the back rest I was leaning against. "Just getting you positioned the way I want you," he explained.

"Cupcake, you can position me any damn way you please," I purred, trying my best not to rut my hard-on against the chair.

I watched as Jett threw away one toothpick and immediately popped another one in his mouth before picking up his machine. "Gonna start with the outline. Since you can't see from there, it doesn't really matter if you want to watch or not. Don't tense up, don't hold your breath. Just try to breathe normally. If you wanna talk, we can talk. If you'd rather go silent, that's fine too. Did you want your headphones or anything?"

"No, I'm good."

"Ready?"

"Let's do it," I said, suddenly not feeling *as* confident as I had five minutes ago.

The buzz of his machine startled me, but the warm touch of his hand distracted me for a brief moment. The first stroke of the ink against my skin took me by surprise. I hadn't known exactly what to expect and the sensation wasn't what I'd call pleasant.

He worked for several moments while I focused on breathing.

"You okay?" Jett asked.

"Yeah, I'm good. It's different from what I was expecting."

"Better or worse?"

I thought about it for a bit. "Neither. Just different. Kinda feels like one of those really fine-point pens writing on a sunburn."

"Yep, I hear it described that way a lot. You're doing great. 'Bout halfway done with the outline. Let me know if you need a break."

I allowed myself to sink into a relaxed state of mind. It wasn't as if I didn't feel the pain against my skin, but I understood now when people said they kinda disappeared into it. I wasn't sleepy by any stretch of the imagination— and the earlier dick issue had taken its leave with the first touch against my skin—but I definitely found myself pulled into a deeply relaxed state.

Before I knew it, Jett's machine stopped buzzing and he was wiping me down with something cool on my inflamed skin.

"You're all done," he said.

"That was amazing. You're quick. And very good, it wasn't super painful at all."

"The area you picked isn't usually very sensitive. You sat really well. Small pieces are quick and easy." He finished everything and launched into his aftercare spiel. "Obviously, if you have any questions, you know where to find me," he said as he finished up directions and handed me a folded piece of paper with cleaning and healing instructions. "That's an open wound, keep it clean. Don't let others be swiping their grubby hands all over it."

"Awww, my little lovebug is so cute when he's possessive," I teased as I sat up on the chair.

"Just don't want to have to deal with an infection, not good for business. Sit there for a minute before you stand up. Don't want you light headed."

Over the next few minutes, I gradually righted myself as I watched Jett clean, sanitize, and organize his station.

"Can a person have an organization kink?" I asked.

Jett snorted. "I've seen your room. Organization is definitely not something you have."

"No, I mean like getting off on watching others be all organized and shit. Because I think I've got that if it's a real thing. How do you make cleaning and straightening your shit look so damn sexy?"

Jett laughed and locked his arm around my neck in a playful headlock. "Instead of Netflix and chill you're down for sanitize and organize?"

"Oh, baby, talk dirty to me," I quipped, not wanting the contact and laughter between us to stop.

For one brief moment, I swore on everything special to me that Jett pressed his lips against my hair and breathed in deeply like he was kissing my head and savoring my scent.

But that was crazy, right?

He cleared his throat and let go of me so fast I would have fallen to the floor if I wasn't still sitting on the edge of the chair.

"Okay, so, we'll talk about your next one once you get an idea of what design you want," Jett said, turning his back on me and messing with a non-existent job on the counter.

"Sounds good. I know the location, just not the design yet."

I followed him to the front where I paid for the tattoo and tipped him generously.

"You don't have to tip me that much," Jett protested.

I shrugged. "You have time for lunch?"

He checked his appointments. "Yeah, next one isn't for a couple hours, I'm good."

"Good. You can use your tip to buy me lunch." Hooking my arm in his, I led us out the front door and waited while he turned the sign to closed and locked up.

"How's the pain? Too terrible?" Jett asked as we walked toward the diner.

"No, it just feels like a sunburn."

"Tomorrow will likely be pretty uncomfortable and the itching as it heals can be kinda intense, but overall, it shouldn't cause you too much trouble."

We enjoyed our lunch together, talking and laughing as if we'd been doing it forever.

Jett went back to the shop for his appointment.

I went to work for my shift.

And I spent the whole afternoon and evening wishing my day with Jett had been my actual date instead of the upcoming one I'd agreed to go on.

With a perfectly attractive, interesting, charming man.

A man who didn't do a single thing for me.

A man who wasn't Jett.

Jett.

The man who ticked every single one of my boxes.

But he's straight and you're still not over the trauma of what Stephon did to you. You swore you'd stay away from straight guys.

Yeah, but that was before Jett.

Despite thinking I needed to move on, I wasn't going to cancel a date—who passes up the chance to get dressed up, have dinner bought for them, and maybe get laid?— but I also wasn't going to purposely look for dates or hookups with other guys.

At least for a while—I'd been wrong when I decided I was ready for that.

I needed to get a better grasp on whatever *might* be simmering between Jett and me.

———

RAYMOND WAS ATTRACTIVE, attentive, intelligent, and kind.

We had quite a few things in common as far as music, food, movies, and hobbies.

He had a successful, stable job.

He lived on his own in a nice part of Midtown.

He had a great laugh, was well-groomed, and drove a fabulous car.

But the only thing I could focus on throughout dinner?

Raymond wasn't Jett.

Jett with his dark hair and serious dark eyes.

His ink...the visible designs and the ones I dreamed of one day seeing.

That stupid toothpick.

His dry sense of humor and the little smirk I swore he saved just for me.

Jett.

"Did you want to go back to my place or yours?" Raymond asked as we exited the fancy Midtown restaurant he'd taken me to.

Neither?

I had no desire to get stuck at his place.

And I really wasn't feeling the date going much further than the enjoyable dinner, but I hated the idea of ending things awkwardly by telling Raymond I wasn't interested.

He wasn't sending up any warning signs.

I wasn't at all fearful of being alone with him.

I just wasn't at all turned on by being alone with him.

"Let's go to my place. I've got an early shift," I lied, "but we can have a drink before I have to head to bed."

I pretended not to see the brief flash of disappointment over Raymond's face.

Damn it.

Why did I have to have Jett on the brain?

Maybe Raymond wanted a bit more than I could offer at that point in time, but getting involved with a guy like him—even if he wanted more and I wanted less as far as a relationship went—would have been a nice change from sporadic sex between long droughts with only my right hand to satisfy me.

But noooooo…

I had to go and find myself obsessed with Jett.

Physically.

Emotionally.

Pathetically.

Pointlessly.

Obsessed.

When we reached my top floor apartment, I thought briefly about mixing drinks, but decided that might indicate more interest than I had. So, I set two pods of coffee to brewing as I gave Raymond a very limited tour of our place.

"This is nice. If I worked in this area, I'd like to live here," he said.

"Yeah, it's a great place. I've got it good because I have amazing roommates."

We settled on the little couch in the foyer of my and Jett's room—I wasn't sure who was home so I avoided the main living area…and I definitely didn't want to have Raymond in my bedroom.

He immediately placed his cup of coffee on the little end table and took my hand. "Leighton, I had an amazing time tonight. I'd like to do it again, get to know you better." The fire in his eyes should have lit me up, but he might as well have thrown a match on wet leaves.

Knowing I should have just told Raymond I wasn't feeling the same, I put my coffee on the floor and let my stupid, lonely, desperate hormones make the decision on my next move.

I straddled Raymond's lap, enjoying the look of sheer surprise on his face.

If I was going to tell this perfectly acceptable man I wasn't interested, I needed to be *sure* there was nothing there.

Three things happened within the next few moments.

First, Raymond gripped my hips and rocked our groins together before snaking one hand up the back of my shirt and pulling me closer for a kiss.

Two, I immediately knew there was no spark. Not even the slightest wisp of desire for the man. Truly, such a shame.

Three, the door opened.

"Jesus, Leighton," Jett grumbled. "My bad. Sorry."

The door *snicked* shut as I froze on Raymond's lap. "Fuck," I mumbled.

Raymond graciously deposited me on the couch cushion and shifted in his seat to face me. "Let me guess, one of the amazing roommates?"

I smiled. "Yeah, that's Jett. He shares this living space with me. I hadn't told him we'd be here, so he was probably just coming in to shower." I stared through the door as I spoke, as if I could see Jett on the other side. My head was a jumble of thoughts—the two most prominent being *no, Jett didn't look disappointed to catch you with another man* and, the one I really wanted to believe, *Jett definitely looked disappointed to see you with another man.*

My date gave a gracious smile. "And can I assume he's the reason you've not seemed super into this date tonight?"

I hung my head. "I'm really sorry, I had a very nice time."

"No worries, it was a fun evening."

"It's pretty much pointless anyway," I said ruffling my hair and reaching to take a sip of my coffee.

Raymond cocked a brow.

"Jett isn't into me," I explained. "We're just friends."

He snorted and stood up. "You need your eyes checked. That man definitely wasn't happy to find you in here with me."

Hope flared to life in my chest. "For real? You saw that? It's not just wishful thinking on my part?"

"For real." Raymond pulled me to stand beside him. "From the look on his face, he doesn't know what to *do* with what he's feeling, but he's definitely feeling." He leaned in and kissed my cheek. "Come on, walk me out. Maybe you can salvage your evening with your man."

"Thanks for being so great," I said as I reached for the door. "I'm really sorry for leading you on."

"Nah, we had a good time. Who am I to stand in the way of potential happiness?"

After giving Raymond a hug and wishing him the best, I paused for a moment to listen to Jett slamming around in the kitchen. I had to guess no one else was home or they would have come out to see what the ruckus was about.

Sensing he wasn't ready to talk at that moment, I left him to his noise making and headed to take a shower.

By the time I walked out of the bathroom, the slamming in the kitchen had stopped and Jett's door was closed.

I needed to talk to him.

Needed to...

Hell, I didn't even know what I *needed* to do.

I just wanted to talk to Jett.

Spend time with him.

Know we were okay.

As I paced my room, lounge pants slung low on my slim hips, hair still damp, I heard the shower start.

I filled the time imagining Jett in the shower.

Naked.

Wet.

Warm water sluicing over his golden, inked skin, running in rivulets down his V lines.

Fuck, I didn't need a damn boner in my pajama pants when I went to talk to Jett. I needed to calm the fuck down.

I gave him five minutes after the shower stopped and his door clicked shut.

And then I left my room, stood in front of his door for a full thirty seconds, and finally knocked with my heart hammering in my chest.

When I got no answer after an embarrassingly long time of standing there, I retreated toward my own room.

Only to hear Jett's door open.

We stared at each other from our doorways.

"You need something?" Jett asked, headphones around his neck, dressed in only the most enticing gray sweatpants I'd ever seen, his skin still dewy and flushed from the hot shower.

"Just wanted to talk," I answered.

Jett nodded and moved toward my room, depositing his headphones on the side table next to the couch.

We stood awkwardly at my door.

"So, talk," Jett said.

"Um, sorry about the awkwardness earlier," I hedged.

Jett's mouth worked as if he was longing to chomp on a toothpick, but he huffed. "No worries, sorry to interrupt."

I sighed. "Nothing to really interrupt."

He cocked a brow. "You didn't like him?"

"Raymond was perfectly nice. Attractive, successful, would have taken me to bed in a heartbeat and likely proposed within six months." I pinched the bridge of my nose.

"But?"

"But my stupid ass is hung up on someone else and no matter how many times I remind myself that certain someone isn't interested, my head and heart can't seem to let it go."

"I'm sorry…" Jett started.

"No, it's not your fault. I didn't mean to make things even more awkward. We just have this weird situation where you're the object of my unrequited obsessed affection, but you're also somehow my closest friend and the person I want to spend time with and tell things to. Blurred lines at their finest." I stretched and yawned. "I just didn't want to go to bed with anything weird between us. I know I said I was going to try to start dating again, but I think tonight showed me I'm better off just hanging with friends and jerking off when the need arises."

We stared at each other for what seemed like a lifetime

before Jett nodded and turned as if he was going back to his room.

But he stopped with what sounded like a frustrated groan and ran a hand through his dark hair.

"It might not be as unrequited as you think and I absolutely *hated* seeing you with him," he mumbled.

For the brief moment it took for his words to sink into my addled brain, I just stared at him. When I could finally move, I grabbed his arm and yanked him to face me.

"What?" I nearly screeched. "Say that again. Please."

Jett took a deep breath and closed his eyes. "I said I hated seeing you with that man and what you're feeling might not be so unrequited."

"Explain," I demanded.

"Which part?" Jett huffed.

"All of it. Why did you hate it? What do you mean it's not unrequited? Am I getting punked? Is this a dream?"

With absolutely no warning, Jett pressed me into the door frame, his hands coming up to cup the sides of my face as his nose nudged mine. He let loose a half laugh, half sob mixed with a moan. "I have absolutely no idea what the fuck is going on, but I think we need to talk."

Before I could say another word, before my brain could process what in the hell was happening, Jett's warm lips were on mine, tentative and curious.

I pulled back a fraction of an inch to look into his eyes. What I saw there set fire to my blood. Jett wanted me. He maybe didn't understand any of it and wasn't sure what to do with it, but he wanted me as badly as I wanted him.

"Kiss me," I murmured against his lips, my arms snaking around his waist and pulling him close.

My request was all he needed. Jett dipped his head, his mouth meeting mine in a slow, sensual kiss that outranked every single kiss I'd ever received all grouped together. He tasted of mint and desire, his lips and tongue exploring mine as his hands split time between gripping the back of my neck and running up and down my bare back.

When we broke for air, I watched his face for the freak out I was sure was coming. When he didn't pull back, just sighed and pressed his head to mine, I took the chance of breaking the spell and spoke.

"What was that?" I stroked his lower back, wanting to rock our hard lengths together—ignoring the fact I could feel his thick cock pressed against my thigh. "Don't get me wrong, it was amazing and I'm down for doing it again and again, just a little confused on where it came from."

Jett snorted. "You and me both. I'm so fucking confused. I don't want to fuck this up. I thought I could ignore it, but seeing you with that guy tonight—wanting it to be *me* you were straddling, *me* taking you on a date, *me* bringing you home and taking you to bed—I realized it's not fair to keep it to myself. Or maybe I'm just a greedy bastard." He shifted, his forehead bumping a bit too forcefully into the door frame as he leaned over my shoulder. "I can't lose you as a friend, but I don't know how to talk about this, do this, figure it out without you, and I'm worried I won't be enough. Worried the messed-up thoughts of right now won't be the same down the road and someone will end up getting hurt."

"Whoa, sweet cheeks, let's start at the beginning. I feel like I just came in at three-fourths through a movie. I need to catch up." I shifted, which was a huge mistake because my dick brushed against his.

We both drew in quick, sharp breaths.

"Can't we just keep kissing and ignore everything else? Put off talking for a while?" Jett murmured at my ear.

Knowing it wasn't the smartest idea, but also knowing it was maybe a chance I'd never get again—yeah, I realized I needed to be making us both think with our heads instead of our dicks, but my dick was talking much too loudly—I rocked our hips together as I brought my mouth to Jett's.

Savoring the slick heat of his tongue and the flavor of his kiss, I whimpered against his mouth when we finally broke apart, both breathing hard. "Kissing all you want to do?"

Jett gripped my ass and rocked his cock into me. "No? Fuck, I don't know. I don't know what this is. I don't know what I'm doing. I just know I want this. I've been wanting this. None of it makes sense except how much I want you."

"Let me take care of you. Later, we talk. That's a must. But for now, you just sit back and enjoy. Can you do that?" I moved us toward my bed.

"What about you? I don't want to seem like I'm using you like that guy you were with back then." Jett let me sit on the edge of my bed, spread my legs, and position him between them, his back to my front.

My eyes caught his in the full-length mirror in front of us. "You're nothing like him. I promise, I'll get as much from this as you will. And we *will* talk about this. Seems like a lot needs to be said and figured out." I nibbled at his ear lobe and breathed in the scent of his freshly showered skin. "But for now, just relax. If I do anything you don't like, just tell me. Nothing has to happen that you don't want."

Jett dropped his head back to my shoulder. "Fuck, I feel like I want it all. I don't even know what that truly means, but if it's with you, I want it."

"Shhhh, I gotchu," I murmured. My head was screaming at me to slow it down, my heart was rejoicing, and my dick was begging to keep going. I let my hands trail down his pecs, tracing a line from his belly button to the low waistband of his pants. "This okay?"

Jett nodded. "Yeah," he mumbled, his words catching in his throat.

"Can I touch you?"

His cock twitched under his pants and he nodded, his eyes never leaving mine in the mirror.

I worked the waist of his pants down, his long, thick shaft springing forth. Part of me wanted to freeze time and savor this moment forever.

Desire to touch him and bring Jett pleasure won out.

Stroking him gently, almost afraid I would wake up from the best dream of my life at any moment, I watched Jett's face in the mirror for any sign he didn't want my hand on him.

Instead, he thrust his cock into my fist with a grunt as he gripped my knees and spread his legs.

"Fuck," he gritted out. "Fuck that's good."

I spit into my hand and returned to jerking his shaft, thumbing through the pre-cum at his slit.

"Kiss me," Jett whispered, his head turned, lips seeking mine.

We kissed, tongues exploring, as he thrust into my hand, my fingers gripping his throbbing cock. My other hand ran up and down, caressing his chest, his abs, moving to cup his balls, and then beginning the journey all over again. I marveled at the varied designs inked into his skin, wanting to trace my tongue over each and every one of them.

The problem with jerking off the guy you've been fantasizing about since the day you met him, watching him in the mirror, his eyes on you as his cock thrust into your fist, is that it was pretty much the most erotic, sensual act I'd ever participated in—probably had more to do with the fact I was experiencing it with Jett than the actual act itself, but still, it was hot as fuck—and my horny ass was nowhere near being able to hold off busting a nut.

So, when I added more spit and Jett increased his incoherent mumblings as he watched me jerk him off, my own balls drew up tight and I knew there was no way I'd escape this escapade without blowing a load in my pants.

"Fuck, Leigh, I'm so close. Gonna come," Jett grunted, almost apologetically.

"Do it, wanna make you come, wanna feel you unload in my hand, smear your cum on your skin," I murmured in his ear. "Come for me."

SEVEN

Jett

IF WHAT LEIGHTON was doing to me was wrong, I never wanted to be right.

I was possibly confused about my feelings toward him, but having his chest and cock pressed against my back, his hand on my throbbing dick, and his sweet mouth whispering dirty words in my ear was the best thing I'd ever experienced and I never wanted to stop.

My nuts ached, begging for release.

"Come for me," Leighton demanded, whispering his dirty, hot words as he stroked me, his eyes caught on mine in the mirror.

My cock pulsed, unloading over his fingers and my stomach, my body convulsing as I grunted my release.

The press and throb of Leighton's dick against my lower back sent sparks through me. Knowing what we were doing was affecting him as much as me made everything seem better...less confusing, at least for the time being...as if we were in it together.

Leighton released his grip on my spent cock and traced

a finger through the trail of cum on my stomach. "That was fucking amazing; you're gorgeous."

I hummed my response. "Haven't come that hard in... well, in ever." It was the truth. Even when I jacked myself off, and especially with the girls I'd been with in the past, I'd never felt so right and satisfied afterward.

"As much as I'd like to just curl up and sleep, I jizzed my pants like a damn teenager, *and* we have things to talk about." Leighton pressed a kiss to my neck. "Coffee and cake while we talk?"

I chuckled. "That sounds good. Can we keep the conversation to ourselves for now?" Julian and Ollie may have known a bit about my unexpected feelings toward Leighton, but I wasn't prepared for a group conversation.

"Sure thing. Let's clean up and meet back in here. I'll start the coffee as soon as I wipe myself off and find new pants." Leighton threw a box of tissues at me. "As amazing as you look covered in spunk in my bed, you need to make yourself presentable or I'll end up on my knees sucking you off when we're supposed to be talking."

My damn dick attempted to twitch back to life at his words. I groaned and Leighton laughed.

Ten minutes later, we settled on the couch in our little foyer area outside our bedroom—avoiding either bed seemed wise for the time being.

Leighton handed me a plate with coffee cake from Cravin'-a-Cup. "Not even stale, I just got it this morning."

We ate and sipped our coffee for a couple minutes. I got the feeling Leighton was about to burst, but he waited patiently while I did my best to gather my thoughts.

Setting down the plate and reaching for a toothpick I'd

tossed on the side table, I rolled the slim wood between my teeth and took a deep breath.

"Sweetie boo?" Leighton asked with a smirk and cock of his brow.

"No," I huffed out, laughing at how easily he broke the tension.

He smiled. "We're friends. I know we just completely smeared all pretenses of lines, but you can talk to me. Sex doesn't have to make things different or bad between us—we'll always be friends."

My heart jumped. "Swear to that. No matter what, friends first." I really couldn't stand the thought of losing him if things between us got too messed up. I wanted *more* with Leighton—although, I wasn't really in a state of mind to know exactly what that meant for the time being—but, more than anything, I wanted his friendship.

"Friends first, always." Leighton took my hand and squeezed.

Grateful for his touch—and mad at myself because I hadn't thought of reaching for his hand first despite how badly I craved the connection—I squeezed back.

"Start with not liking seeing me with Raymond," Leighton suggested.

I shook my head as I thought back to walking in on them. They'd both been fully dressed and nothing more than a casual kiss was taking place, but I'd felt as if I'd been punched in the gut. "I hated it. The moment I saw you with him, I wanted to throw him out the window and have you all to myself. The thoughts and feelings were sexual, but they were also just possessive—like, that's my Leighton and no one else can have him." I huffed out a breath. "Wow, that doesn't sound creepy or anything."

Leighton smoothed a thumb over my knuckles and offered a reassuring smile. "It's okay," he murmured. "Is tonight the first time you've felt this way?"

I shook my head. "No."

"Schmoopy, I'm gonna need more than one-word answers."

"Schmoopy is a hard no," I deadpanned. "No, it's not the first time. It's hard to pinpoint when I started feeling differently toward you. You've been unique and special since the day we met—at first, you were just the only person who didn't seem to give up on me...actually, one of the few who even thought I was worth the effort—so that was new. Then, over time, you became a friend and I realized you were the person I wanted to talk to, spend time with, all that shit."

"Such a romantic sweet talker," Leighton teased. "Go on."

"Even the fact you've got me talking so much—about feelings especially—shows how fucked up I am." I chomped on the toothpick. "Somewhere along the line, the base thoughts of friendship morphed into something more. I didn't even pick up on them at first because my entire life I've assumed I was straight. Never caught my eyes on other dudes, never wondered what being with a guy would be like. Then you came along and my mind started wandering into unexplored territory."

"So..." Leighton started, "are you thinking you might be gay?"

I ran a hand through my hair. "I'm thinking about a

billion things and at least a million of them have no answers, or contradict each other, or bring up at least a thousand more questions."

"Try to explain," Leighton urged.

"When I think about other guys, I don't have any desire to touch them or spend time with them or have sex with them." My eyes met his. "But when I think about *you*, the first thought is of friendship and how much you've come to mean to me in such a short amount of time. Then I'm punched in the face with thoughts of kissing you, touching you, being with you in ways I've never once imagined with another guy."

"And these imaginings excite you?"

I snorted. "Understatement."

"Does that bother you? Are you angry or scared about feeling this way toward me?"

I appreciated Leighton doing his best to be objective. "Yes and no. In a way, I'm angry because these feelings are changing up everything I thought I knew. I guess I'm kinda scared—I *know* my parents would flip out if they ever found out, but that doesn't worry me much. I'd like to think Grandpa would be okay with it." I flopped my head on the back of the couch. "Mostly, I'm just confused. Maybe a bit relieved?"

"Do you wanna talk about that?"

No. What I wanted to do was hold Leighton and sleep for a week. I sighed. "Confused because I don't really understand how these feelings could just crop up out of nowhere—like, you're amazing, but I don't think you're magical."

Leighton's soft snort mixed with a giggle did weird

things to my gut. "I won't take that personally for the time being. You said relieved?"

"Yeah. In a way, the intensity of what I'm feeling toward you helps me to know I'm not broken. All those years of going through the motions with girls, never really understanding what the big deal was, feeling as if I could basically take it or leave it when it came to sex and relationships, then you come along and everything kinda clicked."

"Do you think you might be demisexual?"

I huffed. "I don't know what that means. That's another thing this whole situation has me thinking about —I'm clueless. Like, I've just been going about my life, thinking I was a dud with sex and girls, never questioning anything, and then *boom*. And now I realize I know nothing."

"Are you wanting a label?"

Shaking my head, I rubbed a thumb over his soft skin. "I don't think so. Maybe one day when I understand the labels better or there's one that fits me perfectly, but right now, I think they're more confusing than anything. Unless there's one I'm missing that means *I find girls physically attractive and now that I think about it I find guys physically attractive, but the reality is the only person I have any romantic and sexual interest in is my best friend who I just met a few months ago* then I don't think there's a label for me right now."

Leighton nodded. "I get that. *Gay* was easiest for me, but if I really started digging into my sexuality I think I'd find more specific labels. I don't need to, gay fits for now."

"Can you tell me more about your past with that guy?" I asked. I was tired of talking so much, my verbal upchuck had me physically and emotionally drained, and I needed to know more about what Leighton had been through.

He was quiet for a long moment. "I don't really like talking about Stephon because it makes me look like such a loser."

I tipped his chin up. "Never. You don't have to tell me, but I want to be sure I never do any of the things he did to hurt you."

Leighton snorted. "As long as you don't string me along forever, promising you'll eventually leave your girlfriend—who I didn't know existed until much later—while making me turn my back or cover my face so you can pretend I'm a girl while you fuck me, we're all good."

"Fuck. I'm sorry. That's messed up and he's the biggest loser douche ever for putting you through that."

Leighton shrugged. "I'm the one who allowed myself to be put through it. He just took advantage of the fact I was into him and kept convincing myself he'd eventually come around."

"I feel caught between a rock and a hard place here. I don't ever want to take advantage of you…"

"You could never," Leighton assured.

"I know you've been attracted to me since the beginning," I hedged.

"Not like I kept that a secret," Leighton teased.

"Right. So, I feel kinda like I'm exploiting that attraction—exploiting our friendship even—when I pour out all of my concerns and issues. Like I'm coming to you to learn how to be…whatever this is that I'm finding out about myself…and putting you in a difficult position."

Leighton frowned. "Dimples, unless you're asking me

to marry you tomorrow and move to the suburbs in a house with a white picket fence, three children, and a dog, I don't see a problem."

It was my turn to frown.

He continued. "We've already got a close friendship. The attraction is there. I'm not looking for a serious relationship or settling down at the moment. I doubt you're ready to jump into something serious. We're the perfect friends with benefits scenario."

My heart plummeted. I'd known Leighton wasn't interested in getting serious, but I wanted to be more than just a hookup on repeat for him. "So, just fuck buddies?"

He screwed up his nose. "Nah, we're more than that. I can help you figure things out. We'll keep it low-pressure and casual. We're built on friendship and that won't crumble around us. We can add in sex as another facet and it's a win-win for both of us."

What if feelings get involved? I wanted to ask, because my feelings were already involved. But it wasn't as if I was going to turn down whatever Leighton was offering. I didn't want to go find another guy—Leighton was the reason all of this had been set into motion anyway.

I nodded. "Yeah, sounds good. As long as we swear the friendship thing doesn't get messed up." I wouldn't be able to forgive myself if I let anything fuck up our friendship; he truly meant the world to me.

Leighton stuck out his little finger. "Pinky swear."

I rolled my eyes and hooked my finger with his. "So, how's this gonna work?"

He tapped his chin. "I think we start slow."

I snorted. "Slow like you jacking me off in the mirror after our first kiss?"

Leighton laughed. "Okay, so that was maybe a bit fast for our first time together. Let's just take it slow from here on out. I think jumping into anal the day after our first kiss is a bit too much for something this new."

"Agreed," I said with a chuckle to cover the groan fighting to escape when I thought of being with Leighton in that way. "Kissing okay?" I leaned in close, tossing the toothpick to the general vicinity of the side table as my lips brushed over his.

Leighton's mouth was soft against mine. "Kissing is always okay," he whispered.

By the time we finally broke apart, I was ready to throw slow out the window and take Leighton to bed for the next week.

Instead, we parted ways and he took a tiny piece of my heart with him.

As I lay in bed, wondering if I was making a huge mistake—not the liking Leighton part, but the mixing friendship with sex while not letting him know I had more than casual feelings for him—I couldn't help but smile when the little tap sounded against the wall.

Knock.

Hi.

I returned the single knock.

Knock, knock, knock.

You okay?

Again, I gave one return tap.

Knock, knock.

Good night.

With my heart in my throat, feeling all floaty and weird in ways I'd never felt, I gave two good night taps back and rolled to my stomach.

As sultry images of Leighton's hand stroking my cock danced through my head, I realized with certainty that being with him wasn't causing any stress.

My mixed-up feelings had to do with him, but none of them were directly *about* him—which maybe didn't make a single bit of sense.

All of my feelings surrounding the whole situation had to do with *how* and *why* and *when*, but thinking about being emotionally and physically involved with Leighton didn't give me pause.

Sure, I was hesitant about taking steps further into our physical relationship—I had zero experience with a man and not a great history with girls. But I was also beyond curious about the fun we could have—my imagination was enticed to say the least.

For a moment, I wondered how Julian and Ollie—and the rest of the guys—would react seeing Leighton and me together. Although, Leighton had been pretty clear he thought of this as just a casual extension of our friendship, so maybe no one would really notice the addition of a physical relationship.

Sebastian likely wouldn't say anything. He seemed to be the type who kept opinions to himself unless asked.

Shaw would probably just give his soft, sweet smile and go about his day.

Dean and Lucas—yes, they usually got named together as one entity because they were so joined at the hip everyone assumed they were a couple despite their insistence they were just life-long friends—definitely wouldn't care. They were very much the types to shrug and tell someone to do what makes them happy.

Ollie would definitely have something to say. He was often growly when he felt the need to protect a friend. I had a feeling he'd be worried Leighton was getting back into a Stephon situation. I needed to make sure Ollie understood that the *casual* stipulation stemmed from Leighton's side of things and not mine.

Julian would be concerned for both of us. Outside of Leighton, Julian was the person I considered the closest friend. It was strange to have gone my whole life always feeling like I never fit in, having only my grandpa as a friend and confidant, and wondering why other people had all of these connections while I didn't, only to end up living with a group of guys I'd quickly come to call friends.

Julian would listen without too much judgement and take on the caretaker and advisor role in making sure neither Leighton or I got hurt.

But if Leighton eventually decided he was tired of our friends-with-benefits situation and he wanted to move on with someone else, I'd definitely be the one left to heal a broken heart.

Opting to not dwell on that depressing thought, I let my mind wander to the artwork I'd been working on for the appointments I had over the next few days and sleep soon took over.

EIGHT

Leighton

WHAT IN THE actual fuck was I doing?

The tattoo on my ass wasn't quite through the itchy stage and the sensation was enough to let me know I wasn't dreaming.

So, what in the hell had possessed me to offer casual sex with my until-now *straight* best friend when I knew very damn well I had more than casual feelings toward him?

You know what possessed you. Your horny dick took over and you threw all common sense out the window from the moment you wrapped your fingers around Jett's thick cock.

Fuck.

At the thought of what we'd done, my ass clenched and my dick plumped.

Touching Jett, watching him come apart, knowing I was the first guy to get him off, feeling his warm body pressed against mine as he lost himself and unloaded on my hand was a damn wet dream come true.

And, thanks to my big mouth and tiny brain, I was

now in a situation where I could get Jett off any time either of us felt the need.

As long as I didn't let on I wanted more with him. And since when did I want *more* with a guy? Up until Jett, I would have sworn I wanted nothing more than easy, casual, no-strings sex after the mess Stephon had caused for me.

I was a hopeful dreamer and I wouldn't give up on the possibility of Jett and I developing into something more than casual as time went on. But until he settled into his sexuality, I needed to tread lightly and keep things as casual and easy as possible. Nothing would send a guy running faster than going from *I'm not looking for anything serious, let's fuck* to *I think I fell in love the first days I laid eyes on you, fill me with your babies,* so I had to play it cool.

The last thing I wanted to do was scare him off and lose our friendship.

Or worse, keep the friendship and have to watch him go fuck around with other guys because I'd promised casual and couldn't deliver.

I curled into my warm blankets.

The prospect of consistent sex was promising.

The idea of consistent sex with my best friend was new to me, but no less promising.

As long as I let my horny ass do the thinking and decision making, while keeping my sappy feelings out of every equation, I was certain this new development with Jett would work out just fine.

Good luck keeping those feelings at bay my head whispered to me even as my romantic heart fluttered hopefully as I fell to sleep.

—————

I'D BARELY CLOSED my door after a shower a few days later when I heard a light knock. Jett and I had been keeping things as normal as possible, sneaking kisses here and there, but sticking to *slow* at least for a bit.

"Yeah?" I called, not worrying about being in just my towel because living with seven other guys meant we'd all seen junk before. Plus, I had a strong feeling that none of the other guys had even the slightest interest in seeing me naked—except maybe Jett.

Speak of the devil and the object of my affection popped his head into my room with a sheepish smile as he worried his bottom lip. "You got a minute?"

"Yep, don't have to be to work for a while, but I was already awake so I figured I'd go ahead and shower. You?"

Jett stepped fully into the room. "Yeah, I don't have an appointment until later today, but it's a big one and will take several hours."

So, we both had the morning off.

That was...

Promising.

"What's up?" I asked, yanking on a pair of loose joggers and tossing my damp towel over the back of my desk chair.

Jett, dressed in just basketball shorts, ran a hand through his still-wet hair. "Wondered if you wanted to talk about your next tattoo and maybe get breakfast? If you have time," he mumbled.

My heart soared, but I just shrugged. "Definitely."

Letting on that my poor little homo heart was touched he wanted to spend time with me wouldn't be *casual*.

Jett took a step closer. "Um, thought maybe we could work on that whole casual...uh...*thing* too, if you're interested."

My dick twitched to life.

Fuck.

Had Jett come in to ask me to breakfast *and* initiate sex?

My little straight boy was growing into a fine gay man; I was so proud.

"Boo-bear," I crooned, reaching out and running my hands over his well-defined and highly-inked pecs.

"No," Jett answered with a snort, shutting down the nickname before I could continue.

"Baby bear?"

"No."

"Boo-baby?"

"I'm leaving," Jett deadpanned and made as if to reach for the door.

"No, no, I'll stop," I said, chuckling and wrapping my arms around his neck. "Good morning," I whispered against his lips.

He gripped the back of my head and dipped his head to devour my mouth. Hot, wet, and definitely the best good morning kiss I'd ever had, I let myself melt into the sensation of being in Jett's arms, tasting him on my tongue.

When he finally broke the kiss, he pressed his forehead to mine. "I, um, I think you may have created a monster.

My brain is on overload thinking of all the things I want to do with you."

I huffed out a laugh. "Well, that's a good problem for me to have. I'll solemnly swear to do everything in my power to keep the monster satisfied." Kissing him again, soft and slow—softer and slower than casual truly called for—I smiled against his lips. "From this day forward, I am but your humble sage, spreading my knowledge just like I'll spread my legs."

Jett snorted. "Oh my god, pretty sure *I've* created a monster too. You're enjoying this way too much, aren't you?"

I ran my hand down his ass and pulled our hard cocks together. "What's not to enjoy? Seriously, though, anything you want to do, anything you have questions about, anything at all, feel free to ask. I can either show you, teach you, or we can have a hell of a good time learning together."

Jett nodded. "Wanna show me where you want that next tattoo?"

"How about I show you how good my blow job skills are? Then we hit breakfast." I slipped my hands under the waistband of his shorts. "I'll come by the shop tonight for the tattoo consult." Jett didn't need to know about my fantasy of getting dirty with him in his shop until I had him exactly where I wanted him later.

"That works," he answered, his words husky.

"Sit on the edge of the bed." I gave a gentle shove. "And take these off." I yanked at his shorts and nearly swallowed my tongue when the movement revealed his plump bare ass. "Mmmm, I'm not usually too concerned about a guy's ass, but that is one fiiiine specimen right there, sweet cheeks."

"I feel so objectified," Jett said. "I'm more than just my ass, you know."

For a moment, I almost thought he was serious—the man had such skill with keeping a straight face—but then he bit his lip, his eyes twinkling, and I laughed. "Sorry, you're right. You're a smile that can light up the room..." And send my heart soaring when it's directed at only me. "A fine ass..." I dropped to my knees and nudged his legs apart as I nuzzled my nose against his inner thighs and licked his balls. "And a dick just begging me to choke on it."

Jett's chuckle was tense, laced with desire, as he leaned back on his hands. Taking advantage of the movement, I ran my tongue up the underside of his shaft, focusing on the thick vein and swirling around the sensitive head.

Jett grunted. "Fuck, Leighton, that's good."

"Oh, you sweet innocent baby, I've not even gotten started." I gripped his length, stroking slowly, lapping at the pre-cum leaking from his slit.

Cupping his balls and giving a gentle pull, I lowered my mouth down his cock, loving the way he groaned when his cock head hit the back of my throat.

I wasn't under the impression Jett had never enjoyed a good blowjob—honestly, it took a pretty specific mix of criteria to make a blowjob *bad* in most cases—but I was determined my oral skills were going to be the best he'd ever had.

Perfect suction, perfect spit level—not too dry, not too

sloppy—just the right amount of gentle teeth, and an almost non-existent gag reflex served me well.

Soon, Jett's hand fisted in my hair and his body tensed. I knew he was fighting the urge to thrust into my mouth.

"You can fuck my face," I offered.

Jett grunted and thrust his hips up hard and fast.

Loving the way his hot, silky shaft slid through my lips, I squeezed his balls as he went to town on my throat.

Jett stopped and pushed me away. "Gonna blow, too soon, give me a second," he gasped, fisting his cock and squeezing tightly.

"Lie back on the bed," I demanded. "Wanna show you something. If you don't like it, just say."

Jett eyed me suspiciously through blown pupils, his eyes proof of how drunk on lust he was. He followed my directions and lay back, his thick cock standing nearly straight up, his balls drawn tight.

I slicked my finger with spit before returning to suck his cock. With my slippery finger, I teased between his ass cheeks, brushing over his tight pucker.

Jett tensed, but his pleasured moan filled the room.

"This okay? Can I play?" I asked, my breath hot against his throbbing shaft.

"Fuck, yeah," Jett bit out.

Pushing a pillow under his ass, I spit on his taint and ran my finger through the wetness to slick his hole as I moved back to sucking his gorgeous cock, already addicted to the flavor of him on my tongue.

"You ever experiment with a finger or toy?" I asked, nearly busting a nut when I thought of Jett playing with his tight hole.

"Finger, yeah," he mumbled. "Fuck, Leigh, wanna feel it."

That was all the invitation I needed. As I sucked him deep, I pressed gently against his puckered ring and worked slowly, patiently, as his body opened for me. Knowing I was the only man to breach him, the only man to bring him pleasure in this way, was a heady feeling and one I already wanted to experience again and again.

When his tight, hot body had opened for me, I pushed deep, brushing my finger over that sensitive bundle of nerves, and smiled around his thick shaft when Jett's hips bucked and he cursed.

"Fuck. Shit, Leigh, fuck. Do it again. Gonna come." Jett rocked his hips, spreading his knees wide, his heels digging into the mattress. "Don't come yet, I wanna jerk you off."

Fuck.

As if those words weren't going to drive me to nut in my pants right then and there.

With a final brush of my finger against his prostate, Jett grunted and gave one more thrust, his throbbing cock unloading in hot, thick spurts on my tongue.

He groaned as I swallowed around his pulsing cock head, taking every drop he gave me, loving the salty burst of flavor.

"Come here," Jett demanded, sitting up, his thick spent cock slipping from my mouth as he pulled me between his legs, turning me so my back was to him, my hard cock tenting my joggers. "Wanna watch you in the mirror like you did me."

Jett pulled the front of my pants down below my nuts

and guided my hips between his spread thighs. He caught my eye in the mirror and smirked. "Maybe not original, but is this okay?"

I nodded, longing to jack myself off as he watched, but realizing he needed time to get comfortable and explore. "I've got amazing ideas, you can copy them anytime. Imitation is a form of flattery, right?" I choked on the last word as Jett ran his thumb through my leaking slit. "Shit, honey bunches," I gasped.

"Not a chance," Jett warned, taking his hand away from my dick.

"Okay, okay, just touch me, damn." I groaned when he wrapped his warm hand around my desperate cock. "Please, stroke me. Wanna come. So close."

Jett turned my head to meet his mouth in a hot, wet kiss. "Do it, come for me. Wanna watch you shoot your load."

He stroked me, watching me in the mirror, his eyes bouncing back and forth between meeting mine and gazing at my cock.

"Touch my balls," I begged.

The warm press of his fingers cupping my nuts was all it took.

My cock exploded, long stripes of cum painting my abs, dribbling over Jett's fingers, his hand milking every last drop from my pulsing dick.

For a brief moment, as Jett examined the spunk smeared on his hand, I feared he was going to freak out. Instead, he ran a salty finger over my lips and gripped my chin, forcing me to meet his hungry kiss.

"Only ever tasted mine," he mumbled against my lips. "Like yours better."

We kissed long and slow for several moments before my stomach growled. "As fucking hot as this has been, I was promised breakfast before going off to toil through my day."

Jett laughed. "Yep, ten minutes to clean up and then we'll head out."

About fifteen minutes later, Jett shook his head with a tiny smile just for me as I walked into the living room where he, Julian, Shaw, and Ollie were sitting. "Of course, you turned ten into almost twenty," he said.

"More like fifteen, and it takes time to look this good."

Our eyes met, sharing a secret.

Ollie huffed out a laugh—no malice or judgement in it, just a noise that let on he had a very good idea what Jett and I had been up to.

Julian eyed the two of us warily. His look saying he didn't want anyone to be hurt.

Shaw, as one of the newest and quietest guys in the house, didn't appear to pick up on anything different between Jett and me. He sipped his tea and looked as if he'd do anything to just crawl into Julian's lap and take a nap.

Julian, sitting close to Shaw on the couch without actually touching, didn't look as if he'd mind at all for Shaw to do just that.

Interesting.

I knew Julian was a caretaker at heart.

I knew Shaw had a rough past.

Maybe they'd be good for each other.

If Julian wasn't so hung up on the age thing.

Ollie's roommate, Sebastian—who preferred to be called Bash by friends—came into the room with a mug. He was the oldest of all eight of us—reminded me of a funky, wise old owl—but he looked damn good.

I didn't miss the way Ollie's eyes glued themselves to his roomie; the poor guy needed a bib for how much he was drooling.

They'd look good together, that was for sure.

And they had a lot in common—well, I guess I didn't *know* that, but they both were involved in education, seemed to like a lot of the same movies and music if their conversations were to be believed, and had a similar style—but the age gap between them was also a likely issue.

I didn't know about Shaw—maybe he wasn't into older guys, maybe he didn't see Julian in a romantic or sexual way—but I did know Ollie was just dying to climb Bash like a tree.

Both Julian and Sebastian were probably fighting any attraction to the younger men because of some ill-conceived notion that the age difference was a big deal.

Jett nudged me with an elbow, breaking me from my matchmaking haze.

I needed to stop creating scenarios in my head and just let nature take its course with my friends. If they were meant to be, they'd *be*; they didn't need any interference from me. I was a strong believer in the idea that the universe put people together who were supposed to be together—whether as friends or lovers or *whatever*, I truly believed it.

"You ready?" Jett asked, the toothpick caught between his lips and an eyebrow cocked in question.

"Yep." I turned to the others. "Enjoy your day here while we go wither away at our jobs."

Ollie scoffed. "Whatever. You both love your jobs. Plus, Bash and I have work to do at the center—it's open six days a week if you'll recall."

"I've got a list a mile long to work on today," Julian added.

I eyed Shaw with a smile. "Come on, tell me you at least get to loaf around all day."

He smiled softly. "No, I have a shift later. Lucas and I are leaving in a bit."

"Damn. Okay, well, everyone enjoy their day and don't work too hard. We need to have a nachos and game night soon. Let's make it happen." I hooked my arm in the crook of Jett's elbow as naturally as I took my next breath.

Realizing what I'd done as we reached the door, I tried to pull away with a whispered *sorry*, but Jett tightened his arm on mine as if to say *you're good, stay where you are.*

So, I settled into him, enjoying his warm strength.

"You feeling okay with what we've done in the last few days? Regrets? Freaking out? Reconsidering?" I asked as we headed down the stairs rather than taking the elevator.

Jett shook his head. "I'm good. Thought I'd maybe feel some of those things, but so far, all I've felt is relief. The things we've done have felt so right—I'm still confused about why it took so long for me to figure this shit out... and I don't feel like I'm even a tenth of the way through *actually* figuring anything out...but I don't doubt I'm attracted to you and I definitely enjoy what we've done so far."

We walked into the diner and I knew immediately I wanted a big, greasy burger instead of breakfast.

"I'm pretty sure Ollie and Julian were suspicious this morning," I said as we took our seats.

"Definitely." Jett blushed. "Neither of them said anything to me directly, but the looks they were giving me spoke volumes."

"I'll be sure they know this isn't you using me. They're protective after what happened with Stephon."

Our waitperson arrived with waters. "Are we ready to order?"

"I'll take the breakfast platter, please," Jett said.

"I'd like a burger, hold the lettuce, tomato, and onion. Just pickles and cheese, please. And fries with ranch."

"Perfect. I'll get this right in. We just had a big wave leave from earlier so the kitchen should be pretty quick to get this out to you."

Jett raised a brow, chewing on his toothpick, and smiled. "Look at you ordering your food the way *you* want it. Proud of you."

I shrugged, feeling my cheeks heat. "This really hot guy who happens to be my best friend once told me I should ask for what I want."

"Sounds like a really smart guy," Jett teased.

"Smart, hot, good in bed," I quipped.

Jett rolled the toothpick. "What if I'm not?" he asked, his serious demeanor back in place.

"What?"

He glanced around and lowered his voice. "What if

I'm not good? In bed? Sex in the past has never been hearts and fireworks for me. What if it's because I suck?"

My stupid dick perked up at the thought of Jett sucking, but I ignored it. "Have the things we've done together given you similar vibes as sex in the past?"

He shook his head. "Not at all. The things we've done have definitely been the fireworks variety."

I shrugged. "For me, too. I guess we can't *know* how anything else will be between us, but based on our limited experiences together so far, I have high hopes." I nudged his foot under the table. "And keep in mind, we don't *have* to do anything more than what we've been doing. Full-on anal sex doesn't have to be the end goal. If either of us decides it's not for us, that's okay."

Jett cocked his brow, gnawing on the toothpick. "Did Stephon make you feel bad for not wanting that?"

I shook my head. "No, but he always acted like any other physical act wasn't *real sex* and that's just not true. Sex is whatever you and your partner want it to be."

"Do you *want* anal? It's something you enjoy?" Jett asked in a whisper.

"With the right person, it's amazing—Stephon was *not* the right person, which is likely why I preferred to stick to the other stuff—but it's not the only way to experience pleasure." I stopped short of admitting how badly I wanted Jett inside of me. My desire to be with him that way had a lot less to do with physical pleasure and a whole lot more to do with an emotional connection that went *way* past casual.

"Do you only bottom?" Jett asked.

"Just depends. I consider myself vers, but if given the choice, I prefer bottoming."

Jett's cheeks flushed. "I don't even know what I'd prefer. I mean, I've loved what we've done."

I pressed my knee against his under the table. "No worries, that's why we're doing what we're doing so you can figure that stuff out."

Jett's finger brushed against mine on the table and he opened his mouth as if to say something, but our food arrived and he snapped his mouth shut.

We spent the entirety of our breakfast in easy conversation.

I fought the urge to wrap my arms around his neck and kiss him silly when we parted ways on the sidewalk. Instead, I told him I'd come to the shop after my shift so we could discuss the next tattoo.

"Later, pookie bear," I said.

"No," Jett replied. "Hard no."

"You're no fun."

"Have a good shift," Jett said with a smile in his words, his pinky finger brushing mine just slightly as he turned toward his shop.

Would Jett want to hold hands at some point?

Holding hands didn't scream casual sex.

Ugh.

I was so screwed.

For someone who swore they weren't ready for anything *but* casual sex, I'd quickly gone and fallen head first into a hole filled with a lot more than casual feelings for Jett.

I mean, it wasn't really surprising considering I'd been

gaga for the guy since Day One, but it kinda shocked me how quickly I'd gone from thinking I wanted just casual to realizing I wanted more than that with Jett. Maybe *just casual* with other guys seemed like a way to protect myself from getting hurt again, but my heart knew Jett was different and it was all for exploring *more than casual* with him.

Seeing as how Jett agreed to our little set-up under the pretense of easy and casual, I definitely needed to keep all that feelings shit under wraps so as not to scare the man away.

I whistled happily as I headed toward the coffee shop. A day full of caffeine, sweets, and chit-chat sounded like a great way to pass the time until my consult with Jett.

NINE

Jett

I WAS ABSOLUTELY EXHAUSTED by the time I cleaned up from the four-hour session with one of my best clients. I checked my phone and smiled when I saw a message from Leighton saying he was on his way.

I was so hopelessly fucked over him.

I'd felt out of place most of my life. I'd been the loner, the kid who was never good enough for my parents, the guy who just never really fit in no matter how hard I tried or didn't try.

I'd questioned a lot in my life.

Why did my parents have me if they didn't even seem to want me around?

Why did I never seem to click with the people around me?

Why did relationships always seem so drab, lackluster, and disappointing—both emotionally and physically?

But I'd never once questioned my sexuality.

Then I met Leighton and everything seemed to just fall into place.

Leighton wanted me around. Hell, even my new roommates seemed a lot happier to see me than my parents ever did.

After twenty-five years of never really connecting with a lot of the people around me, I'd found myself living with a group of guys I could actually call friends.

And while I still wasn't completely sure what was up with my sexuality, I knew for a fact I was attracted to Leighton on both an emotional and physical level. In fact, had I not agreed to keeping things casual, I was pretty sure I'd have already asked him to make our little arrangement more official.

But I couldn't do that because he'd made it clear he wanted easy and casual.

So, I'd take what I could get for now. No matter that I'd never really wanted anything serious with anyone I'd dated. No matter that what I felt for him in such a short time far surpassed anything I'd ever felt for anyone else.

I'd enjoy the casual sex with my best friend for now and hope for more as time went on.

And prepare my heart for devastation if and when Leighton ever decided he wanted something more with someone else.

Part of me felt like it should be weird how easily I'd accepted my attraction to Leighton—how easily sex with him had just seemed like second nature—but another part of me argued everything was so easy because it was so *right*.

I didn't have any for-sure answers, but I knew I felt something for Leighton and I was just happy to have him in my life any way I could get him.

The moment Leighton walked into my shop, I could tell something was wrong.

Every single sexy thought I'd had about getting him on my table, my hands on his smooth, pale skin went flying out the window when I saw the drawn look on his face, the distance in his eyes.

"What's wrong?" I asked, immediately flipping the door sign to closed and engaging the locks.

"Started getting a migraine about an hour ago. Took my medicine, but it's a doozy."

"I didn't know you get migraines. What can I do?" I took his elbow and turned him to face me.

"Not a lot. The visual disturbance was bad and lasted a longer time—which usually means it's going to be a bad one—but that part is gone now. I'm just kinda nauseous and I'm dreading the headache part. I need to drink a lot of water, take another pill, and sleep—I went ahead and asked to switch shifts tomorrow because I know it's going to be a rough one." He gave me a weak smile. "Didn't want to miss our consult. Had all these ideas for getting dirty in your shop, but don't think that's on the agenda now."

"Forget that shit," I bit out.

The wounded look on Leighton's face made me cup his cheek and kiss his forehead. "I had the same thoughts. I just meant we're not messing with a consult when you're sick. Come on, let's get you home and comfortable."

"But my tattoo..." he trailed off, his words already sounding weaker.

"You live with your artist...hell, you're fucking your artist..." Damn, I liked the sound of that. "I'm pretty sure figuring out a good design and placement can happen almost any time and place."

Leighton leaned into my chest with a sigh. "I hate these damn headaches. The pain will be bad and then the day after will almost be worse."

I hugged him close. "I only have one short and easy appointment tomorrow, I'll keep you company while you ride it out."

"I'll be terrible company, mostly just sleeping."

We headed out the back door, Leighton's arm hooked through mine as he kinda shuffled as if his whole body was already struggling.

"No worries. I'll be there."

I got him up to the apartment and made him drink a bottle of water with his second pill.

"Can only take two—usually just need one which is how I know this one is gonna be bad—but hopefully it will help ease the pain," he explained.

"Would a warm shower help?" I asked.

"Probably not for my head, but I'm gross after a long shift, so I'd feel better getting clean."

"Are you dizzy or anything? I can get in and help?" I offered.

Leighton grinned—even feeling sick, his smile still lit me on fire—and closed his eyes. "Fucking headache. Hot guy of my dreams offers to shower with me and I can't even take advantage. I'm not dizzy, but I'm definitely not gonna pass up the chance to get naked with you—as long as you know there's no way I can get it up with the way I'm feeling."

"Noted," I said. "Definitely wasn't trying to jump your bones when you're sick."

"But we can get dirty in the shower another time?" Leighton asked, wincing against the bright light in the bathroom.

"For sure. Is the light a problem?" I'd never known anyone who had migraines. Not because they were so rare, just because I didn't have a lot of people I knew well enough to know about their health issues.

"Yeah, bright light, loud noises, sometimes smells."

I clicked off the bathroom light and helped Leighton undress. "Go ahead and get in, I'm right behind you. I'll crack the door so a bit of light comes in."

The water was just this side of scalding when I climbed in, but Leighton was standing under the stream as it poured down on his head. "You okay?"

"Yeah, this feels good. Won't make it stop—once I start getting one this bad, there's nothing to do but ride it out—but it's somewhat of a relief." He reached blindly for something. "Can you hand me my shampoo?"

I grabbed his bottle and poured a dollop in my palm. "Here, let me do it. Just relax. Is the headache bad yet?"

Leighton moaned as I massaged the shampoo into his hair, my fingers kneading his skull. "Fuck, that's good. We *have* to do this when I'm not sick so I can drop to my knees and suck you off while you massage my head."

I laughed and kept working my hands over his head, willing my dick to behave itself. A boner while washing my sick friend's hair would have been totally inappropriate.

"The headache is building. I'd like to think I'll be asleep before it's too terrible."

"Well, tell me when you're done and we'll get dried and curled up in bed."

By the time we were out of the shower, dried, and dressed, Leighton was shivering and I could tell the pain was bad.

"Come on," I said, guiding him to my bed. "Climb in. I'm going to hang our towels and get some water. You need anything else?"

Leighton froze at the edge of my bed. "You said you don't like the idea of people in your bed. I can go to mine."

"No, I have no problem with *you* in my bed. When I said that, I meant people I didn't know. People I didn't *want* there. Sick or not, I want you in my bed. Come on, crawl in. I'll be right back."

I made sure the towels were hung up, rushed to the kitchen for water, let a curious and concerned Ollie know what was up, and almost sprinted back to my room. I made sure my phone, charger, and tablet were next to the bed and gently joined Leighton under the covers.

"You want another blanket?" I asked, pulling him close, his back pressed to my front.

"No, I'm good." He shivered and moaned.

"Shit, I didn't even think, is touch a problem? Will it make things worse to have me all cuddled up on you?" I started to pull away, scared to cause him any more pain.

"No, it's perfect. I think you're the sweetest, most caring, compassionate man I've ever known and I'm so grateful you're here." Leighton snuggled into my arms.

"Thank you for taking care of me. Hopefully I'm a bit better when I wake up."

I'd definitely never been called all of those things; I wasn't exactly sure how to take the compliment. "Is there anything I should watch for that would constitute an emergency?"

Leighton shook his head. "I've never had to go to the ER or anything. If I start puking and not be able to keep liquids down, probably take me, but I don't see that happening. Just hold me for now. Gonna try to sleep."

Luckily, he fell asleep pretty quickly. I had a feeling the medication maybe made him drowsy. Any thought I'd had of drawing or surfing social media while he slept was doused when I realized I couldn't really move without the risk of waking him up. So, I held him, marveling at how good it felt to have him in my arms even when it was for something as shitty as a migraine.

I wanted this.

I wanted Leighton in my arms, in my bed, in my life… for *real*.

How did I tell him that?

Julian's words from a while back came to mind. *Tell him.*

But what if I told him and he freaked out? Leighton had specifically said Stephon messed him up so much that he wasn't ready to do anything close to a real relationship.

But are you going to be happy with just fuck buddies?

I breathed in the clean scent of Leighton's damp hair.

I figured I didn't really have a choice. I didn't want to be with anyone else. I didn't want to go back to being *just friends* with Leighton—even though I knew that was a possibility down the line—and I didn't want to lose him.

So, I'd keep my growing feelings to myself.

How in the hell had I managed to uncover a dormant... bisexuality? Homosexuality? And end up attracted to and falling for one specific man who was so fucked up by an asshole ex he wasn't sure he could risk his heart again.

Suddenly, anger filled me.

Fuck Stephon.

It wasn't fair that he'd messed Leighton up so badly that we couldn't have something special.

The worst part about it was Leighton had wanted something special with Stephon and the asshole had gone and ruined things.

Now, because of the past hurts, Leighton thought he didn't want something special despite the fact I was right there ready to do the whole *real* and *special* thing.

But does Leighton know that? No, because you haven't told him. *Tell him the truth and let him make the decision. Non-communication is one of the quickest ways to mess shit up.*

Tell.

Him.

My eyelids drooped. Emotionally and physically, I was exhausted.

I needed to be in a better state of mind when I decided on what to do about my feelings for Leighton.

And he was in no position to be dealing with me messing with our situation.

Things could wait.

I'd waited twenty-five years to finally find a place where I fit and a person I connected to on a deep level. Telling him I was attracted to him and agreeing to casual sex had been a huge step. I could wait a bit before letting him know I lied about the *casual* thing being okay.

Leighton slept straight through the night and only roused when I got up to pee the next morning.

"What time is it?" he mumbled, his sweet voice sleepy and definitely still not himself.

"Early. I'm gonna use the bathroom and go back to sleep for a while. You need anything?"

"Gotta pee. Need water. More sleep."

"You can go first," I offered.

Leighton sat up slowly as if testing the level of pain in his head.

Hovering, because I wasn't sure what to do, I waited on him to use the restroom before shuffling back to bed. I handed him the water bottle from the night before.

"Thanks," Leighton said, draining the bottle.

"Sleep some more. My appointment is at ten, so if you wake up and I'm gone, that's probably where I'm at. You're off today?"

Leighton nodded. "And tomorrow. Good thing too, because the throbbing, excruciating pain is gone, but now I'll spend today exhausted and in a fog with a different pain in my head—like it's been beaten black and blue with a baseball bat."

I winced. "Damn. That sucks. You need anything?"

He was already drifting off and shook his head. "I'm good."

After the bathroom, I crawled back into bed—completely cognizant of the fact I'd never shared my bed with anyone and I knew I was already addicted to having Leighton in it.

A few hours later, I gathered my clothes and crept from the room to take a shower. Ollie, Julian, and Shaw were in the living room when I entered. Bash was in the kitchen pouring himself a cup of coffee.

"He okay?" Julian asked.

"Yeah, says the first round of pain is done and now the second part starts." I grabbed a bowl and fixed myself cereal.

"A lot of patients describe the day after a migraine subsides as a migraine hangover," Shaw said. "There's a lot of treatment for migraine, but there's still a lot of unknown surrounding it."

"He's sleeping. Says he'll probably do a lot of nothing today." I took a big bite of cereal. "You guys seen him get one of these before?"

Ollie nodded. "Yeah, he's had two bad ones like this one in the time he's lived here, I think. Pretty much wiped him out for two whole days. I was freakin' out the first time he got one because he just casually said, 'Fuck, I can't see your face, hang on, I need to take some medicine.' The not being able to see would scare the shit out of me."

"From what I've read and heard, it's not so much a blindness type not being able to see, it's more a visual disturbance. Waves, black spots, portions of what they're looking at being blocked out. Some people get the visual aura and some people don't. A lot of times, if a person can take their medication at the first sign of an attack, they can often curb the severity," Shaw said.

I didn't miss the look Julian had on his face—kinda like awe—as Shaw spoke.

"He says his medicine works a lot of the time, but if it's going to be a bad one, the medicine will only slightly help and his only option is to ride it out. Sucks. I feel bad for him, wish there was something I could do to help."

Julian pulled his eyes from Shaw. "I think you're probably helping more than you realize just by being there for him."

Fighting the urge to beat my chest and declare there was nowhere else I'd rather be, I took a final bite. Finishing off my breakfast, I stood. "I've got an appointment, but it's short and sweet—kinda just a fluff piece, but money is money—I'll be back in a bit. Someone gonna be here if Leighton needs something?"

"Ollie and I have work at the center, but we'll be here for about an hour still," Bash offered as he settled in the recliner with his coffee.

"I'll be here until this afternoon," Shaw said.

"Sounds good, I'll be back long before that." I grabbed my phone and the shop key. "Oh, Leighton's in my bed if you need him."

Four pairs of eyes landed on me, but no one seemed surprised as I waved and headed to work.

Two hours later—seriously, the prep and clean up took longer than the actual piece—I'd been to the little grocery and made up a care package for Leighton before stopping off at Cravin'-a-Cup to get myself a large black coffee and him a London Fog. I wasn't sure how he was feeling, but I knew it was his favorite drink.

Leighton was still in bed when I got home, but he was awake and had showered if his damp hair was any indication.

"Hey," I said as I walked into the room. "How you feeling?"

"Worn out—which is always so weird, like how does a headache do so much damage? But I'll survive."

I sat on the edge of the bed. "Is there any kind of medication to help you not get them at all? I feel like I've seen commercials or something."

Leighton shrugged. "I don't get them often. A lot of the preventative treatments are more for those who get them multiple times a month, like five, ten, or more—poor bastards—but since I only get maybe one or two every month or so, I opt for more of a rescue medication than a preventative."

I leaned over and kissed his temple. "Well, I hated seeing you so sick."

Leighton's hand cupped my cheek and pulled me closer for a long, slow kiss. When I shifted to deepen the kiss, the bag crinkled. "Shit, I'm gonna make a mess. Here, this is for you."

His eyes brightened and he bit his lip. "You got me something?"

"I mean, it's not anything huge, just some stuff I thought you'd like while resting today." I handed him the bag and the drink.

He sniffed the drink. "London Fog? That's my favorite."

"I know."

His eyes brightened and he looked as if he wanted to say something, but just took a sip of the drink instead. "Oh my god, that's good. Hits the spot just right." He looked into the bag and squealed. "These are my favorites too."

"I *know*," I teased. "I wasn't gonna get you stuff you don't like."

"But how do you know I'm addicted to mint lip balm, Kit Kat is the bomb, and rainbow goldfish are superior to all other goldfish?"

I shrugged. "I guess I've paid attention. It's not like it's a secret. You smear that lip balm on almost as often as I pop a toothpick in my mouth. I've seen Kit Kat wrappers littering your room like an urban grunge art display. And even if I didn't know you liked the rainbow fish, I'd get them for you anyway because the colorful ones remind me of you."

Leighton grinned, his eyes suspiciously shiny. Did a migraine make a person more emotional? "Fuck this headache. I wanna do all kinds of dirty things to you when you talk that way."

"We have time," I said. And we did. While Leighton seemed to be lodged in my heart as if I'd known him a lifetime, we really were fairly new to the friendship as a whole, and extremely new to the physical aspect of what we had going on. While my body was *very* interested in doing all the sexy things with Leighton, intellectually I knew we didn't have to rush anything.

We settled into bed for an all-day and all-night marathon of snacks, drinks, mindless television, and naps.

We were doing absolutely nothing, but I loved each and every moment we spent together.

The next week proved to be challenging. Our schedules didn't match *at all* so we barely saw each other.

For an entire week, we stole quick kisses here and there as we were able.

We sent texts multiple times a day.

Leighton had a string of early, *early* shifts while I had a whole week of late, *late* appointments. It sucked, but life did that sometimes.

He was always asleep when I got home. I was still sleeping when he left for work.

We grabbed every available moment, but it wasn't enough for anything more than a quick chat, a few kisses, and promises of dirty fun when our schedules matched better.

Finally, *finally*, Leighton texted me to let me know he was done with the earliest shifts for a while and asked if he could come by the shop that afternoon for the consult.

I'd been fantasizing about getting him alone in my shop for so long, I'd nearly forgotten he actually wanted another tattoo and we needed to talk design, placement, and price.

I checked my appointments, told him a time, and settled in to work on a kind, chatty client with a smile on my face as I looked forward to Leighton's arrival.

By the time I flipped the door sign to *Closed*, I was hyped to see Leighton and pretty much wanted to say fuck the tattoo while I ravished his pretty mouth in the back room.

Instead, I locked the front door, turned the shop playlist to something fun, and sat on the chair near the backdoor to wait for Leighton's arrival.

When a quick three knocks sounded on the door, I immediately thought of our nighttime wall knocks and what three knocks might mean. I'd missed the secret taps on our shared wall while we'd been so busy, but more than anything, I just wanted time with Leighton in my bed again.

I yanked open the door, tugged him inside, and locked the door behind him in less than five seconds. Not soon enough, I had Leighton in my arms, his arms wrapped around my neck, and my face buried in his neck while he chuckled against my chest.

"Mmmm, I'm happy to see you too, sunshine," he teased, sighing and melting into me.

Without even taking the time to weigh whether I liked the nickname option or not, I tipped his chin up and nuzzled my nose against his. "Missed you," I said, words husky and very close to being highly *un*-casual.

Leighton brushed his lips over mine. "Me, too. Got spoiled seeing you all the time. I've missed my hang-out buddy."

My heart dropped slightly. Right. Hang-out buddy. Friend with benefits. Convenient and casual sex. That's what Leighton wanted and needed, and that's what I was for him.

I definitely needed to remember that.

Seemed as if I'd gone from being fine and dandy on my own with no connections to meeting Leighton and getting greedy.

We could have fun.

I could figure out my shit.

Learn some things.

Enjoy time with my best friend.

And not have to let it get weird or jumbled up.

Yeah.

Totally.

Leighton licked at my lips and I grunted, covering his mouth with mine and slipping my tongue inside. He tasted of sweet cinnamon and coffee, and I wanted to strip him naked and lick him from head to toe and back again.

"So, how about we get this tattoo figured out...I feel like more fun things are just around the corner," Leighton whispered, his words holding a world of promise.

"Stretch out on the chair," I told him as we moved to my station.

I grabbed my tablet and Leighton got comfortable on the chair.

"Okay, show me where you're wanting it first."

Leighton's eyes caught mine and he licked his lips, reaching for the waistband of his jeans. "You have all your clients strip their pants off for you, peaches?"

"No. And no. But you're not most clients. Underwear, too."

"Well, I should hope not." With his jeans around his thighs, Leighton worked his underwear down slowly, his half-hard cock the center of my attention as it came into view.

"Show me the area you're thinking," I said, stepping closer, gripping my tablet as if it would help me control my hands from wandering.

Leighton pushed his shirt up and ran his hand over his abs before tracing a finger over the pale, smooth skin of his lower left abdomen, just above the junction of his thigh. Licking my lips, I moved my eyes back to his as he spoke. "Thought right here. I was thinking something bright and colorful. Maybe a peacock feather? Or maybe just a colorful design you create?"

"Can I take a picture for location reference and work on a few designs for you to look at over the next week?"

Leighton nodded. "As long as I know you're the only one looking at the picture."

"Of course," I said, snapping a few pictures—keeping all the intimate parts conveniently cropped out.

"So, if we're done, I guess I can pull my pants back up and we can head home?" Leighton suggested in a voice that sounded as if that was the very last thing he wanted to do.

I tossed my tablet onto my backpack before running my hand from Leighton's cheek to his abs to the area he'd said he wanted his tattoo, loving the darker hue of my skin against his.

"Or, you could maybe keep your cock out and let me try my hand at giving the first blow job of my life," I offered, sure I'd screw it up somehow, but not doubting in the least how badly I wanted to taste him.

"Fuck," Leighton moaned. "Yeah, hot lips, I like that idea so much better."

"No," I grumbled about the nickname as I ran a finger over his now-hard shaft. "You wanna lean against the edge of this chair or sit in my rolling chair?"

"Right here," Leighton answered. He swung his legs over the side of the procedure chair, planting his feet on the ground and leaning back on his elbows, his cock bobbing proudly from a neatly trimmed thatch of dark blond hair.

I pushed my joggers down just far enough to tuck

them under my balls and stepped between his legs, bringing our hard cocks together as I leaned in and kissed him. "I might be really bad at this."

"A hot, wet mouth on my cock is gonna have to screw up monumentally to even hint at being bad. Keep to minimal teeth and adequate slickness and all should be good."

"Noted. Tell me if it's not good. I wanna know what works for you and what doesn't." I pressed a final kiss to his lips and dropped to my knees, nipping and sucking his skin as I made my way to his leaking cock.

I'd never paid much attention to other guys' dicks before, but I liked Leighton's very much. Shorter than mine and not as thick, but still what I'd consider an average size. I found my mouth watering as I anticipated the weight and flavor of him on my tongue.

"Heads up," Leighton warned. "I may have been getting off to this exact fantasy so much that I won't last long once you get me in your mouth. If you're not into cum on your tongue or swallowing, pull off when I tell you I'm close."

I nuzzled my nose into the hair at the base of his dick. "Is it okay if I don't know what I'm into just yet?"

"Yep, just wanted you to have fair warning." His hand ran through my hair. "Now, work at your own pace, but when you're ready, please fucking suck me."

His breathy, desperate words spurred me on and I gripped his shaft, loving the way it felt in my hand as I brought my other hand up to tweak his nipple.

Leighton squirmed and I smiled up at him, licking my

lips. I kept my eyes on his as I moved to cup his balls, stroke his cock, and lick his slit.

He closed his eyes and moaned, encouraging my oral exploration. With the taste of his pre-cum on my tongue, I opened my mouth and took his cock head in, my lips closing around him as I swirled my tongue around the smooth head.

Knowing what I liked when getting sucked off, I continued to fondle his nuts, teasing a finger every so often over his taint, and took his dick deeper into my mouth.

With Leighton's fingers gripping my hair and the heaviness of his cock on my tongue, I found a bobbing rhythm, loving the slide of his smooth, taut skin between my lips.

The empty shop filled with the dirty, sloppy sounds of Leighton's cock fucking in and out of my mouth, his soft whimpers, and me breathing heavily through my nose as I worked to not gag on his prick.

"Fuck, Jett, I'm close," Leighton warned.

I hummed around his shaft and reached down to stroke my own cock. I wanted to taste him, to feel him explode on my tongue.

Jerking myself with the same rhythm as my mouth on Leighton's dick, I tensed when my balls drew tight. Squeezing myself hard, I waited until Leighton gave a final thrust between my lips, his cock pulsing as his thick, warm cum spilled onto my tongue. With the flavor of his release filling my senses, I groaned around him and gave into my own orgasm, spurts shooting over my fist and dribbling to the floor.

Rising to my feet, I pressed our still-throbbing cocks together and pulled Leighton close for a hot, salty kiss, sharing his flavor with him as I savored his unique taste.

Thinking back to what I'd just done, I couldn't help but smile.

"What?" Leighton asked.

"I wasn't sure if I could give a decent blow job, but you totally shot your load. Guess I wasn't half bad." Honestly, I was supremely proud of the fact I'd gotten Leighton off with my first ever blow job.

"Sweet cheeks, that was amazing. So good, for real." He smacked a kiss against my lips. "Now, take me home so we can sneak into the shower together and clean up the spunky smell."

I chuckled. "Sounds good. Let's go."

TEN

Leighton

WHETHER BY CHANCE or some finagling on our part, Jett and I ended up with fairly comparable schedules over the next several weeks.

And it was absolutely glorious.

Never let it be said that good times with someone you're close to isn't the perfect cure for what ails you. Not that anything in particular was *ailing* me, but you get the picture.

Jett and I spent time together and time with friends, and barely a day went by that didn't find us kissing, touching, and often times more.

We hadn't yet taken any steps to move further in our sexual relationship. I'd let Jett set the pace on that and he seemed to be enjoying what we had going on so far, which was fine by me.

Not that I was going to protest if he ever wanted to take things further.

I definitely had major fantasies about getting that

gorgeous dick in me, but not getting to that point wasn't a deal breaker.

My biggest concern at that point in time was how head-over-heels I was for the man I'd coaxed into bed with the promise of nothing serious, no-strings attached, casual sex.

My feelings were absolutely eating me alive—so maybe something *was* ailing me—but I wasn't willing to lose him by telling him I'd gone and fallen in love with him. It wasn't fair to him to pull a bait and switch. And I greedily didn't want to give up on what we had until it was absolutely necessary.

If I had my way, we'd still be pretending things were casual in five years as we walked down the aisle. I mean, hell, we already lived together and spent the majority of our time together. Why not make it casually official and build a life together?

I snorted at my idiotic thoughts.

Jett wasn't even completely sure of himself as far as sexuality just yet. Based on his history with females compared to his extreme exuberance in the bedroom with me, I had to think bi, pan, or gay for sure—if I had to guess on an actual label, maybe demisexual since he didn't find himself sexually attracted to a guy until my fabulous ass walked into his life.

But I digress, my point was Jett was just learning about himself. Not only had I promised him just casual—in fact, I'd convinced myself and him that casual was all I could handle after Stephon fucked me over in every sense of the word—but I doubted Jett was ready for life-building with me or anyone else at that moment.

"Hey, you planning on burning that meat?" Ollie asked from beside me, a bag of tortilla chips in hand.

I pulled myself from my jumbled thoughts and glanced down at the huge skillet of seasoned beef I was stirring. "Shit, no." I turned the burner off and moved the skillet to the side.

The eight of us had finally found a time that worked for *all* of us to hang out with food and games. Jett's grandpa was coming over and we had a nacho bar, drinks, and a brand-new box of totally inappropriate answer cards for a popular fill-in-the-blank card game we all enjoyed playing.

"Drain that and cover it. We'll be building the nacho bar soon."

Ollie had seen something on social media and decided we needed to do the same with our nachos. His plan involved foil on the kitchen island, tortilla chips spread out, and all the toppings piled on top. Then we'd just stand around the island and gorge ourselves on nachos while we enjoyed drinks and company.

In theory, it sounded like a not-too-terrible idea, but I was withholding my opinion until I saw it in reality.

"Well, I need to shower and dress before people get here—and by get here, I mainly mean emerge from their rooms, but still, I need to get ready." I patted Ollie's cheek. "Please, sir, may I be excused from kitchen duty?"

He chuckled and batted at my hand. "Yes, but don't take too long getting ready."

"First, it takes time and skill to look as good as me. Second, being fashionably late is totally acceptable."

"Yeah, well, if I find out you're late to the party because you're fucking Jett…"

I bit my lip, trying to contain an excited smile.

As fate would have it, Jett walked through the door at that exact moment. How I knew it was him when I couldn't even see the door was another indication of how far gone I was over the guy.

I waggled my brows. "Plenty of time. Don't wait for us. But make me a drink even if I'm not here."

With a quick wink and a wave, I made a bee-line through the apartment, following Jett behind our closed door.

Jumping on his back and kissing his neck, we both laughed as we fell to the couch in the lounge area of our rooms.

"How was your appointment?" I asked, tucked comfortably on his lap.

"No complaints. Design was my own, guy sat still, didn't talk much, tipped well. I think he'll come back— hopefully tell some friends." Jett leaned in and kissed me. "What about you? Ready for the party?"

"Yeah, should be fun. Grandpa's still coming, right?"

Jett chuckled. "Yeah, he seems excited. He's bringing a friend and they're getting an Uber so they can both drink."

"Aww, that's cute."

"How much time do we have before we need to be out there helping?" Jett's words were gruff and suggestive.

"Well, I just spent an hour in the kitchen helping Ollie prep, so he can do without me for a bit. Why? Got something in mind?"

"Thought maybe we could get each other off, shower, and then join the party." Jett's hand traveled up my thigh, sending shivers through me.

"I like that plan. Like it very much."

"Then get naked. I don't care where or how, but I want your dick and I want to come," Jett murmured against my lips.

"Fuck, my little sweet potato," I groaned.

"Definitely not," Jett growled.

"Tater?"

"God, no."

"Tater tot?"

"Do you want to fuck around or not?" Jett threatened.

I laughed. "Fine, fine. I'll work on nicknames later." Standing, I stripped my clothes off, tossing them to the side as I checked to be sure the door was locked.

Returning to the couch, I found Jett shirtless and working his pants down his firm thighs.

"Mmmm, is that for me?" I asked, straddling his knees and gripping his long, thick cock.

Jett gripped my hips and positioned me so our cocks rubbed together before taking both shafts in hand and stroking, his thumb brushing through the pre-cum on our slits.

"Wanna watch you ride my cock someday, but not until we have more time and privacy. Can you get off like this?"

I leaned in and kissed him, plunging my tongue between his lips as I rocked my hips, loving the friction of our cocks in his big hand. "I could probably come just from kissing you."

We fell into an easy rhythm of thrusting hips, frotting cocks, and exploring tongues. His hard thighs under me, one hand teasing at my hole, and the scent of our sex between us nearly overloaded my senses.

With absolutely no warning, Jett grunted, wrapped me in his arms, and stood up before making his way to the bed in his bedroom, the door kicked closed and locked behind him.

My back hit the cool mattress.

Jett followed me down and my legs spread for him. "Wanna see you under me, watch our cocks together when I make you come."

"Fuck, baby, yes," I moaned, not even caring if he liked the term of endearment or not.

Jett's arms snaked under my arms, his hands locking on my shoulders as he pumped his hips, our cocks hot and hard together. "Damn, Leigh, I wanna fuck you so bad. Wanna feel you around my cock."

Fuuuuck.

Damn stupid party.

"Want that too," I gasped, losing myself to the pleasure of Jett's hard body against mine. "Fuck, Jett. I'm so close."

He growled in my ear, his breath hot and heavy on my skin as my balls drew up tight. "Do it, wanna know I made you come."

Orgasms with Jett were always amazing—especially because he always seemed in awe of how good we were together, and because he was also always so proud of making me come—but being with him in the most intimate situation we'd ever been in had my body yearning to fall apart.

Jett's thrusting hips faltered and he groaned against my neck. "Fuck, Leigh, I'm gonna come."

The moment I felt his throbbing cock pulsing warm stripes of cum between our bodies, I lost it. My dick exploded, shooting my load, our frotting cocks mixing our releases together.

Jett collapsed against me, his lips pressing kisses against my neck as our bodies trembled.

"Fuck," Jett huffed as we came down from our high.

"Yeah," was all I had the energy to say.

"Maybe we skip the party and just nap," he mumbled.

I chuckled. "Ollie would come find us and drag our asses to his nacho bar."

"Truth. Fine, let's shower."

We spent the next fifteen minutes in warm, soapy bliss as we washed, touched, and kissed. My body hummed, my heart soared, and my brain screamed *danger, danger* as I gave up on all hope of keeping whatever was between us *casual* on my part.

An hour later, stuffed on nachos—Ollie's idea had worked out well—and margaritas, we all trooped up to the rooftop for our game.

For a moment, as I made another trip up to the roof with the last pitcher of margs, I paused to watch Jett.

Ever-present toothpick between his teeth—although, I truly thought he used it less and less these days—black joggers, plain gray t-shirt, dark ink on his olive skin, and a smile that seemed to come easier each day, Jett was an absolute vision.

And he was *mine*.

Well, scratch that. He was fucking around with me.

I only dreamed of him being *mine* for real.

"So, you and Jett, huh?" Lucas asked.

I jerked my head in his direction, nearly spilling the pitcher in my hand. "What? Oh, yeah, we're just fucking around; friends with benefits and all that." It was no secret Jett and I were involved physically and close friends, but I hadn't let on to anyone about my true feelings—at least, not on purpose.

Sure, Julian and Ollie maybe had an inkling, but that was because they'd known me for longer. Lucas was one of the newer roommates and we really hadn't gotten a chance to get to know each other.

He smirked and gave me an *oh really* look. "Man, you two look at each other like you're the only ones in the room. I do a lot of people watching at the bar and I know *just fucking around* versus something deeper."

"And?" I attempted not to sound hopelessly breathy *and* snotty at the same time.

"*And* I'm telling you, the way you two look at each other is a lot more than just fucking around."

My adorable little homo heart got all swoony, fanning itself and batting its lashes, but I had to play it cool. "Nah, Jett's just figuring some shit out. We're tight, but it's nothing serious."

Lucas cocked a brow. "Well, you can keep telling yourself that, but I promise you, I've seen the look in both your eyes when you're looking at each other, there's something more there. Maybe don't be so set on casual that you lose out on something you both definitely want."

Letting Lucas's words sink in, I gave a quick little nod

as he walked away and found Dean. I watched the way the two of them interacted and scoffed to myself. If anyone needed to admit there was something between them, it was Dean and Lucas. Those two were fucking oblivious to what they had.

Or maybe *they* weren't oblivious.

Did one of them feel toward the other the way I felt toward Jett, but didn't know how to approach it with the other?

Even if I decided to come clean to Jett about the way my feelings had morphed—and honestly, it wasn't as if my feelings changed *after* we started hooking up. Noooo, I'd gone into this whole casual thing knowing damn well I was all up in my feels over the guy.

So, how did I tell my best friend that not only was I in love with him, I'd known beyond a shadow of a doubt that I wanted more with him since day one? How did I tell Jett I'd been lying to him this whole time? While he was attempting to figure out his shit, believing me, letting himself enjoy what he thought was just no-strings-attached and easy, I was using him to fuel my crazy stupid dreams of love and a future and doing life together.

Yeah, right. Sure, *that* would go over well.

I pulled my pathetic brain from my thoughts of unrequited love and sashayed the margaritas to the table amongst cheers and laughter for my arrival with more drinks.

We settled down for a very serious not-at-all-serious, raunchy game filled with tears of laughter over the extreme hilarity. Grandpa Nelson and his buddy, Milton, joined right in and the gathering was a huge success. I knew we'd be repeating the evening whenever we could work our schedules around it.

When our cheeks hurt from laughing so much and our buzzes were just this side of too much, sweet Shaw disappeared for a moment and returned with a bakery box filled with Cravenwood's best cupcakes.

With big thanks to the quiet man, his cheeks flushing at the praise, we dove into the confectionaries with gusto.

Seriously, nachos, margaritas, cupcakes, and laughing. What more could you want with a big group of friends. Cravenwood—and our particular apartment—was truly the best.

"Soooo," Bash started and glassy, sugared-up eyes turned his way. "Do you all remember when I asked if you'd be willing to get background checks on file in case I ever needed assistance at the ed center?"

Nods and murmurs around the group indicated we recalled.

"Well, I appreciate you all getting those done and it's time for me to call in a favor." Bash finished his drink and placed the cup on the table.

"We've got a fieldtrip to the zoo coming up," Ollie explained. "We could really use a few of you to go with us and be in charge of a group of kids."

After the date was announced and schedules were consulted, it was determined that Julian, Shaw, Jett, and I would be chaperoning the zoo trip.

We cleaned up the rooftop area and made our way back to the apartment. Once Grandpa Nelson and Milton were tucked safely in an Uber, the eight of us chatted for a bit before making our way to our private quarters.

Just as I had changed clothes and started to make my way to Jett's room, Julian emerged from the shared bathroom and pointed toward Jett's door. "Forgot to ask him about that lock at the shop, the one that keeps sticking. Told him I'd take a look."

Panicking, and not wanting to let on I'd been hoping to get a bit of action, I nodded and acted as if I'd just been heading toward the bathroom anyway. "Oh, right. Well, g'night."

"'Night," Julian said, knocking on Jett's door as I closed the bathroom door behind me.

Washing my face, I wondered momentarily if Julian was conspiring to keep Jett and me apart. Would Julian do that?

Staring at my gray eyes in the mirror, I shook my head. No. Julian definitely wasn't the type to sabotage something like that.

While I brushed my teeth, I reminded myself of the *take it slow* concept we'd started this whole situation with. Since we'd just blown our loads with the sexiest frot session I'd ever experienced, I figured it was safe to say we could wait a bit before anything else happened.

Didn't make me pout any less as I crawled into bed, sad to be missing out on cuddling in Jett's arms. We hadn't taken to sleeping in each other's beds every night, but we often fell asleep together and I definitely took advantage of the snuggle time.

I think being wrapped in Jett's arms was one of the top things I'd miss when our little friends-with-benefits situation came to an end.

Knock, knock, knock.

My heart stuttered in my chest.

Despite *knowing* he meant, *You okay*, I stupidly couldn't help but think of how badly I wanted his taps on our wall to mean *I love you*.

I gave a short tap back.

After a short pause where I told myself not to go to his room, Jett tapped out *knock, knock*.

Good night.

I returned the message and rolled to my side, unsure if I'd ever been so happy, content, scared, and confused in my entire life.

———

"FOR FUCK'S SAKE," Jett mumbled as we followed our ragtag group of kids along the path through the rainforest which led to the sloth exhibit. "Did their parents give them caffeine and sugar before dropping them off for this trip?"

I chuckled. "You're not supposed to say fuck around kids."

"They aren't listening. They're too busy yammering away and burning a thousand calories a minute because *They. Never. Stop.*"

It was true, our oddball little group of kids—six in total, two girls and four boys—had been on full-throttle since we got off the Cravenwood Education Center bus at the zoo that morning.

Our six children had appeared more wound-up than any of the other kids and I had a feeling Bash and Ollie were laughing their asses off at our expense.

Don't get me wrong, our group wasn't poorly behaved. They were just on a level ten that didn't seem to be coming down any time soon.

The two girls were super quiet, but they wanted every sign on every enclosure read to them. One of the boys had the cutest—but *loudest*—little froggy voice and he'd spent most of the day boisterously announcing each and every movement the animals were making.

Two of the other boys were twins, but they seemed to be as different as night and day. One was best buddies with the froggy-voiced kid, the other seemed to hang more with the quiet girls.

The other three boys rounded out our own special brand of *variety*. The slightly older of these three seemed bored and not thrilled to be at the zoo. The middle of the three spent the *entire* day talking about the farting and other digestive habits of every animal we encountered. Seriously, the kid was a walking encyclopedia on all things animal digestion, poop, and farts.

The youngest and cutest boy of our group had a song to sing to each and every animal. He also included a bit of a dance with each song.

All of the kids had brought a lunch so we'd met up with the others for a picnic under a canopy, but they'd also brought money and we'd promised them an ice cream stop after a visit to the sloths.

"You're good with them," I said, not exaggerating. And also not surprised the kids had been in awe of Jett since they'd first met him.

Me too, kids, me too.

Jett snorted. "I guess kids don't know I'm the loser to avoid."

"No, kids are usually good judges of character. They saw you, thought you were cool, and decided you were their buddy." Truly, the kids had been all enamored by Jett from the first moment. "Kids know good when they see it." I hated that Jett still thought of himself as an unlikable loner. So what it had taken him a while to find where he fit best? That didn't make him less deserving of friends and feeling welcome.

"I don't know if I've ever been so tired in my life. We've probably walked like six miles," Jett grumbled.

I checked the mile tracker on my watch. "Around four," I corrected. "We'll take a break with the ice cream. Then we'll really only have time for the dolphin show and a couple stops as we make our way back toward the front to meet the bus."

The ice cream was messier and a lot more entailed than just stopping for a sweet, cool treat. Having the kids with us made everything ten times longer and took ten times more effort.

But they enjoyed the snack and we enjoyed a chance to rest, so it was worth it in the end—despite the sticky hands and faces.

The dolphin show was packed and our little group squeezed onto a front bench on the second level, a railing right in front of us—our whole crew had been adamant they didn't want to get wet in the splash zone seats...all for different reasons...and Jett and I hadn't had a single reason to argue with them.

"I can't see," the shortest girl complained. "Can I sit

on your lap?" she asked Jett, going right ahead and climbing right on.

"Um, sure," Jett sputtered, helping her get situated. "Better?"

She nodded happily, pointing to where the dolphins were swimming in their enclosure.

"I wanna lap," the tiniest boy exclaimed, launching himself onto my legs. "I'm too short."

The other kids didn't seem to mind only having the benches to sit on, so we settled in and thoroughly enjoyed the show.

Jett made mention of how the show had changed a lot from when he'd seen a similar one as a kid, and I noted the same.

"Used to be more of a circus, sideshow type thing where the animals were treated as property, just doing tricks. Now it seems a lot more focused on their well-being, conservation, and preservation," I murmured in his ear as the trainer explained how they'd recently rescued the youngest dolphin and used his natural instincts in his training.

Jett nodded in agreement. "Not a bad thing, just different from the show I remember watching."

The kids were enthralled, however. Aside from squeals of happiness and exclamations of delight, it was the easiest and quietest part of our day.

By the time we trekked back to the bus, I was ready for a shower and bed, *stat*. The drive back to the ed. center started out loud and boisterous, but soon fell silent as most of the kids zoned out or fell asleep.

Once we'd gotten everyone unloaded, parents were

starting to arrive. One of the little girls ran up to two men and excitedly told them about her day at the zoo while pointing toward Jett and me.

The two men smiled and waved, but the girl led them over to us.

"Hi, Mila had a great time today. She says you two were good grownups to go to the zoo with," the taller man said.

"High praise from this one," the shorter, older man said. "Sounds like you two are good with kids. We love ours, but I don't think I could have done a whole day with that many kids at the zoo."

"It was an experience," I said. "I'm glad Mila had fun."

"Do you two have children?" the older man asked.

"Oh, no, we just helped our friend by being chaperones," I answered quickly.

"Shame, good looking couple like you. Do you want kids?" the man pressed on.

"Jessen, leave them alone," the taller, younger man chastised. "Sorry, he's always trying to play matchmaker."

"Oh, um," I stuttered.

"We don't have kids. Not sure about what the future holds," Jett answered smoothly.

While I picked my jaw up from the ground, we waved to Mila and her dads.

"Sorry about that," Jett groused. "Figured a little white lie to some guys we'll likely never see again was the easiest way to get them to go away."

Like an arrow to my heart, his words reminded me that Jett and I weren't a couple.

Just.

Friends.

Friends having great sex, but friends all the same.

"Yeah, no harm, no foul," I said, burying the hurt and idiotic hopes of someday being an actual couple with Jett. I wasn't sure about kids, but the couple part sure sounded fabulous.

And stupid.

So.

Stupid.

"Let's get home. I'm exhausted," Jett said.

We said goodbye to Bash and Ollie, who unfortunately still had work to do before they could leave, and headed toward the apartment.

As we walked in the gorgeous breeze and sunshine, I absently curled our fingers together when Jett's hand brushed against mine.

"Sorry," I muttered, dropping his hand.

"It's fine," Jett answered. "I like holding your hand." He took hold of my hand and entwined our fingers again. "If you're okay with it?"

I nodded, my heart soaring as it once again tried to sort out whatever we had going on.

"Just don't let me fall," Jett murmured as his hand tightened on mine.

My brain whirled a thousand miles a minute with thoughts. What the hell had he meant with those words? Don't let him fall? Fall how? Fall in love? Fall in with me? Fall into something bad?

Or was it just a random, meaningless comment in a somewhat awkward situation?

We arrived at the apartment and I forced the scrambled thoughts away.

After checking the mail, we made our way to the elevators after an unspoken agreement that we'd done way too much walking that day to take the stairs.

"You wanna shower while I grab some food?" I offered.

"You grab food then jump in with me," Jett suggested, leaning down to kiss me and hug me close. I was learning Jett was quickest to let down his guard and get cuddly when he was tired.

Seven minutes later, I had ordered food to be delivered with instructions to just leave it by the door. Locking our door, I stripped from clothes I knew smelled like sweat and animals before climbing into the shower.

Jett's arms immediately wrapped around me. "I'm so tired. Don't think I can do anything right now."

"Same," I murmured into his chest. "Who knew dealing with kids all day was so exhausting. Don't know how Ollie and Bash do it."

"To be fair, they've had time to build up their stamina. And I think the zoo is always going to be tiring—with or without kids—we just got a double whammy."

"When we aren't so tired, we're getting down and dirty, honey bunches."

"No," Jett mumbled against my lips. "About the name, not the down and dirty. I'm good with that. Can I…"

"Can you what?" I asked, my words breathless, my heart picking up speed in my chest.

"I wanna fuck you," Jett answered, gruffly. "Wanna be inside you."

My dick tried to perk up. "That can totally be arranged."

Fuck. I wanted that so bad.

An hour later, full from the food I'd ordered and dozing off to whatever movie we'd turned on, I smiled as Mr. Neat and Organized took our mess to the kitchen.

"I can go to my bed," Jett suggested when he returned to my room.

"No reason if we've got plans in the morning," I answered around a yawn, stretching out on my mattress and fighting the urge to get all swoony as Jett climbed in beside me.

"Mmmm," he whispered against my neck. "What kind of plans?"

I chuckled. "I believe you mentioned wanting to fuck me?"

He grunted. "Fuck. Yeah," he groaned out. "You're okay with it?"

"Baby doll," I paused and laughed again when Jett bit my neck.

"No."

I rolled my eyes. He was no fun with the nicknames. "I'm more than okay with it. As long as you can promise me you want to fuck *me* and I'm not a replacement for a girl or just any hole you can get inside." My gut clenched, remembering how badly Stephon used me.

And me being stupid and naïve enough to let him.

"Never," Jett answered quietly against my temple.

Despite wanting the cuddles and convo to last longer, I couldn't fight the exhaustion washing over me.

We were both asleep within minutes.

I woke before Jett the next morning and carefully climbed out of bed to take advantage of some prep time in the bathroom. By the time I slipped back into bed, Jett was stirring.

"No fair, you snuck a shower and I smell like sleep," he murmured against my neck, licking and kissing.

"I had a few things to take care of before…"

Realization dawned on Jett's sleep-marked face. "Ohhh…" He worked his lips and teeth as if desperate for his toothpick. "In that case, can I have five minutes?"

"You can have anything you want. I want this to be good for both of us, so do what makes you the most comfortable."

Jett scrambled from the bed.

Just over five minutes later, he was back, smelling all clean and minty.

When he crawled into bed and pulled me close, kissing me like he'd missed me for a month, my heart went crazy and my head screamed warnings.

But it was too late.

There was no doubt in my mind I was lost for this guy.

"This isn't just…" Jett mumbled against my lips.

"What?" For one crazy moment I thought maybe he was going to say what we were doing wasn't just casual fun for him either. Thought maybe he'd say he felt more for me than just friendship.

"Nothing we've ever done has been me pretending you're a girl. I need you to know that. I'm not messing around with you because you're all I can get or because I want to imagine being with a girl." He nuzzled my nose. "Not trying to sound conceited, but I could get pretty

much any girl I wanted if all I wanted was a quick fuck—
they never stayed around long after that—but that's not
what I want."

"What do you want?" I asked in a strangled whisper.

"You. Never been more sure of something in my life.
Everything we've done feels right."

I wanted to ask him if just the sex acts felt right or if
the being together pretty much like a couple also felt
right, but I was afraid of the answer.

Afraid to see hesitation on Jett's face.

Afraid he'd laugh it off and tell me it was probably best
if we just stick to the friends-with-benefits situation.

Afraid to know I was good enough to give him
experience with gay sex, but not good enough to be more.

"I know we agreed this was just easy and fun," Jett
said, "but I just wanted you to know I've never imagined
you being a girl."

That was the moment when I should have come clean
and told him I was feeling anything but casual about him.
Been honest before he slid into me, invading my body as
much as he'd invaded my heart.

But I couldn't do it.

Remembering Stephon's excuses and lies. The sweet
nothings that now turned my stomach. The promises of
more.

Jett wasn't Stephon, but I couldn't bring myself to
ruin what we were doing—not just at that moment, but
in the grand scheme of things. If I brought it up right
then, there was a chance Jett would get weird and I
couldn't risk it.

Not because I was so desperate for a fuck—okay, let's

face it, I *was*—but because I didn't want to face the future without my best friend if I went and made it weird.

It wasn't smart.

It wasn't fair.

I'd hopefully come to my senses and fess up sooner rather than later.

My head *knew* I had to be honest with him.

My heart just wanted a little bit more time.

Jett went on. "I'm maybe new to all of this and still not one hundred percent sure of who I am, but *this*," he gripped my ass and pulled our hips together, "this doesn't make me question anything—at least not any more than I was already questioning."

"Good to know," I murmured, shimmying out of the shorts I'd slipped on after my shower and reaching for the waistband of Jett's boxers. "Now," I whispered against his lips, "fuck me."

Jett groaned and wrapped his arms around my waist, deepening the kiss.

Being tangled up with him was always perfect. Protected, wanted, savored—that's how it felt to be with Jett. And my poor little homo heart wasn't letting go of hope that maybe one day *loved* would be on that list.

Jett broke from the kiss and pressed his forehead to mine. "Fuck, I didn't think about logistics here. What do we need?"

I chuckled against his mouth. "Lube is a must. I mean, *yeah*, spit will do in a pinch, but lube is always better. Condoms are something we should discuss."

Jett cocked a brow.

"Don't get me wrong, condoms aren't up for

discussion with other guys I've been with. I was likely stupid enough to go without if Stephon had mentioned it, but he insisted on using them—thank god." I ran my hand up and down Jett's arm. "I would have told you long before now if my sexual health was a worry—all of my screenings have been negative."

"Same here. I mean, I haven't been to the doctor for a while, but I had a full work-up last time and no sex since then."

"Soooo…" I hedged.

"Is going without an option?" Jett huffed, his gorgeous face pinking. "I guess I hadn't thought that far ahead. Is that something you want?"

I cupped his face in my hand. "I want what you're most comfortable with. But I also want you to know that condoms should be a must with anyone after me." The words were barbed wire shredding through my heart. "Until you're in a trusted, committed relationship, always insist on condoms."

Jett's brows pinched together, but he nodded. "I trust you and what we're doing." He swallowed and worried his lip. "Is there a way that works best for you?"

I rolled him to his back and straddled his waist, his rigid cock nestling between my ass cheeks. "This work for you?"

Jett gripped my hips, licking his lips as he traced his thumb over the sensitive skin where my next tattoo was going, and nodded.

"Perfect," I said, leaning down to press a kiss to his lips before working my way down, licking, nipping, kissing his neck, chest, and abs before swirling my tongue around his cock head. "But first," I mouthed against his shaft, moving down to his balls, and then tonguing his taint, loving the way Jett bucked his hips. "Pull your legs back," I instructed.

Jett hesitated just long enough for me to worry.

"If anything ever makes you uncomfortable, just say and we'll stop."

He shook his head. "Just never been in this position. Or this...*act*. It's new. Don't know if it's uncomfortable, just feel really exposed."

"If you don't like it, we don't have to do it," I promised.

Jett nodded and spread his legs, pulling them back with hands on the back of his thighs. I licked my lips before sliding my tongue over his hole, loving the way he grunted and thrust his hips.

"Fuck, Leighton," he growled.

"Good?"

"Yeah."

I returned to licking around the tight ring of muscle, swirling my tongue over his pucker, pressing into his hole while Jett cursed and grunted.

When I swiped over his sensitive skin once again, gripping his rock-hard shaft and stroking at the same time, Jett made a distressed sound and shifted away from me.

"Sorry," he panted, "but that was about to end way too soon. Don't get me wrong, coming that way would be great, but I had other plans if you're still okay with it."

"Snookums," I drawled and moved myself up his body to straddle his waist again.

"Definitely not," Jett said, his eyes on fire, a sexy smirk dancing on his lips.

I rolled my hips. "You don't like?"

"The position is great, the nickname not so much." His hands caressed up and down my thighs and he worked his lips as if searching for his toothpick.

"You okay?"

"Yeah, just kinda worried I'll suck at this."

"This position is great because I'll be doing most the work," I said with a wink as I reached for the lube in my side drawer. "You just provide the pole and I ride it while you look all hot and sexy."

Jett's hands squeezed my thighs. "You look amazing like this." He ran a finger over my leaking slit and reached up to smear pre-cum on my bottom lip before yanking me down into a hot, messy kiss.

Pulling away several moments later—only because my balls were drawn up tight and my greedy ass was *begging* to be filled—I pumped lube into my palm and reached behind me to coat Jett's cock and my hole, fingering myself open as I pushed the slick liquid inside.

Shifting myself so Jett's cock head was pressed against my opening, I worked myself down his shaft inch-by-inch, hissing as he stretched me open a bit at a time. When my ass rested against his upper thighs, I paused a moment to allow my body time to adjust.

Jett's dark eyes locked with mine and his fingers gripped my hips, his chest heaving. "You okay?"

I nodded. "You feel fucking amazing, just been a while." I gave an experimental roll of my hips and moaned as pleasure washed over me. "Fuck, baby," I whimpered. "You can move."

Jett pumped his hips tentatively and I fell forward, my hands resting on his pecs. He gripped my hips harder and thrust upwards, impaling me with his hot, slick cock. "Fuck, Leigh, that's amazing. Fuuuuck..."

I sat back up, loving how deep he was, how he filled me. Rolling and grinding my hips, his bruising grip holding me tight, I rode him, my hands resting on his as my leaking cock bobbed over his abdomen.

"Fucking hell," Jett grunted, his hands moving to my chest, knuckles trailing down my stomach, big hand fisting my cock and stroking. "So fucking perfect."

Raising my arms, grasping my fingers behind my head, I continued the rocking roll of my hips for several moments until Jett took hold of my hips again. "Hold onto the headboard," he demanded.

The movement had me leaning forward as Jett bent his knees, planting his feet on the bed before pumping his hips up, hard and fast.

"Fuck, Leigh, this is going to be over embarrassingly fast."

I whimpered as his pistoning cock slammed into me over and over. "Do it. Wanna feel you come in me."

My words seemed to be enough to send Jett over the edge. He growled, held fast to my hips, and slammed his dick deep into my ass. I rode his pulsing cock, loving the feeling of his load painting my hole.

A moment later, his chest heaving and cheeks flushed, Jett urged me forward. "Come here, move up."

"What?" I asked, still in a daze from watching him come apart knowing I was the first guy he'd ever fucked.

"You didn't get off," he said, one hand trailing through my slick crack and the other gripping my cock.

"It's okay, you don't have to..."

"Want to," he said before sucking me between his lips, pressing his tongue against the underside of my shaft. "Give it to me."

I whimpered, rocking my hips as I watched my cock disappear between his lips.

When his finger slipped into my wet hole, pushing his leaking load back into my body, I lost any control I'd pretended to have. I spurted hot cum onto his tongue, groaning as he swallowed around my throbbing cock while finger fucking me.

"Fuck," Jett said when he'd taken everything I had to give. "That was fucking amazing."

"Pookie bear, you have no idea," I teased, shifting to curl against his side as we both came down from our high.

"Don't even think about saddling me with that name just because I'm in a post-sex daze," Jett mumbled, a smile on his voice.

I chuckled and we dozed for a bit before dragging ourselves to the shower.

We both had shifts to get ready for despite wanting to just laze about in bed all day.

"That was okay, right?" I murmured against Jett's lips as the hot water rained down on us.

"So very okay," he answered before kissing me deeply.

ELEVEN

Jett

Not surprisingly, given how easy our connection had been from the beginning, Leighton and I fell into an easy routine of friendship and fucking.

Yeah, on my side of things, it was a lot more than that. I think it had been more than that since the first day he'd waltzed into my shop. But since Leighton didn't want *more*, I enjoyed what we had going on, and did my best not to think about what would happen when he got tired of fucking around with me and moved on.

Aside from work—and even then, we popped into each other's shops at least once a shift—we were pretty much joined at the hip. The guys all knew we were fucking around—and gave us plenty of shit about our lack of noise control at times—and I'd gotten several comments from them about how Leighton and I didn't seem only casual. One of these days, I feared I was going to snap and tell them I *wished* it wasn't just casual.

I'd been working over a lot of thoughts in my head regarding my sexuality. I still sometimes wondered if I ever would have recognized my attraction to men without Leighton. It was hella confusing because I *now* knew I found men attractive, but I definitely *only* wanted to be having sex with Leighton. Wanted only him in my bed, holding my hand, calling me stupid nicknames.

So, I'd decided, if I'd been looking for the most accurate label, I'd choose to call myself a gay demisexual. But for the most part, I didn't really need or want a label, I just wanted Leighton.

And it was a complete and total mindfuck to know I *had* him, yet I really didn't, did I? He was a daily presence in my life—truly the best friend I'd ever had…pretty much the *only* friend I'd ever had—he made me laugh, held my hand, helped me discover my true self, and brought me more pleasure than I'd ever known—both physically and emotionally.

But he wasn't really *mine*.

And maybe it made me a greedy bastard, but I wanted that.

Wanted to call him mine.

Wanted what we had to be more than just fucking around.

I *knew* my parents would pretty much disown me— even more so than they'd done years ago—but that didn't bother me in the least.

I wasn't sure how Grandpa would take it, and that part *did* bother me somewhat. Not in a way that would make me reconsider who I really was, but just in a way that hurt my heart. I wanted to think Grandpa wouldn't care, but a tiny part of me warned he might.

But that was a bridge to cross if and when Leighton and I were ever more than just fuck buddies.

Just the phrase made my gut clench.

If Leighton moved on, if he found someone else to mess around with—or worse, get serious with—there was no way I could sit idly by and just be cool with it.

Did I want him to be happy?

Of course.

Did I want him happy with someone other than me?

Selfishly, one hundred percent no.

And if Leighton moved on, where did that leave me?

My heart was maybe new to all of this, but it had no doubt Leighton was my person. There was no one else for me.

Period.

With Leighton, I was *me*. My heart and mind were at ease. I was settled. I was home.

No one else had ever been that for me.

Leighton was my perfect match—after a lifetime of square pegs in round holes.

He was my missing piece—the one I'd known was missing, but hadn't realized how badly I needed.

My soul mate—the connection between us...even back when I was kinda annoyed by him...was something I wasn't sure I could even describe to anyone who'd never experienced the same kind of pull.

Even without the sexual side, he was all of those things and more.

But sex with Leighton?

Damn.

Sex had never been earth shattering for me.

Kinda just something to get through, something to do because it was expected, something I'd been taught I should want and enjoy.

Sex hadn't been *bad* per se.

It had felt good, but it was always something I'd found myself zoning out of. Looking down at a pretty girl under me and feeling nothing but the desire to finish and leave. Doing my best to stay in the moment as a girl bounced on my dick when all I really wanted was for it to be over. Avoiding situations where sex would be expected because I just couldn't get into it.

Looking back, I probably should have been wondering about my sexuality, but it hadn't even crossed my mind. I'd been so conditioned to think I wasn't good enough— for parents, for peers—I automatically assumed sex was just another one of my failures.

But then Leighton stormed into my life. With or without sex, he'd wrecked me, but he'd also turned sex upside down for me.

With him, I never wanted sex of any type to end. Or even as it ended, I was thinking about the next time. My brain swam in sensory overload when I thought of how his body felt against mine.

His hip bones under my hands.

The plump, soft skin of his ass.

His lean, defined chest and abs.

His long, toned legs wrapped around me.

Those gray eyes staring back at me as I fucked into his body.

The slight coffee and cinnamon scent of his hair when I nuzzled into him after his shift.

The way he shivered when I kissed the sensitive spot on his neck.

His soft whimpers as he thrust his cock between my lips.

The bell above my door yanked me from my completely unfortunate—based on time and location—daydream about Leighton. Quickly realizing I'd been fantasizing about my man instead of getting ready for my appointment, I gave a wave to my client.

"Give me just a few to finish some prep and we'll get started."

"No problem, man. Gonna have a smoke while I wait." He grabbed the cigarette from behind his ear and headed back out the door.

Once he'd disappeared, I adjusted my disappointed cock and moved to retrieve my tablet and the design I'd printed out to show the client. We'd make whatever changes he wanted, get the stencil transferred onto his skin, and get down to business.

While I often enjoyed clients who wanted to zone out and listen to music, I was glad this one—Curt, a repeat customer—usually wanted to chat. I needed the distraction. Needed to focus on my work rather than obsessing over Leighton.

Ninety minutes later, we took a break. Curt needed a cigarette.

In the past, before I stopped smoking, I would have been right there with him. Not gonna lie, the scent of tobacco—which had once made me crave a smoke—kinda turned my stomach. These days, I opted to stand away from the smoke he was blowing, gnaw on my toothpick, and check my texts.

I couldn't help the smile when I saw Leighton's message to let me know he was coming by the shop after his shift.

I shot a text back telling him how sick this design was looking and I'd see him later.

As Curt and I returned to my station and settled back in for the completion of his tattoo, a peaceful warmth washed over me.

I was happy.

Content.

No longer just making my way through life as a loner.

I had friends.

I had a new business well on its way to thriving.

I had Leighton.

But all of it could come crashing down in a heartbeat if he found out how I felt about him.

True, the friends and the business would still be there.

And I knew better than to build my entire future on one person.

But still…

If I lost Leighton, I'd lose a part of me.

We'd sworn our little tryst wouldn't affect the friendship, but I was no longer sure I could return to being just friends with him when I'd tasted his lips, held him in my arms, felt his tight heat around me.

Maybe you should talk to Leighton, let him know your feelings have changed. Maybe his have, too. Honesty is the best policy.

I knew it was for the best, but like a kid psyching himself out before a flu shot, the anticipation of the unknown—of the potential pain—was just too much. I wasn't sure where to start, how to even approach the subject. Instead, I'd simmer away in my pathetic love stew, longing for something I couldn't have.

You could maybe have it if you'd just talk to him.

Before I could acknowledge the persistent nagging in the back of my head once again, Curt started telling me about a funny story from his kid's preschool class, effectively pulling me from the cacophony of thoughts swirling through my head.

An hour later, we were at the front counter while Curt paid and we chatted about what he wanted for his next piece. Promising to show off my work to all his inked and wanna-be-inked friends, Curt gave a wave and headed out the door.

I had about an hour to clean up before Leighton would likely arrive, so I switched the sign to *Closed* and fell into an easy, methodical cleaning routine.

When my phone buzzed, I smiled, assuming it was Leighton. He didn't often call, usually opting for a text or just speaking to me in person, but I wasn't averse to hearing his voice.

The number was unknown on my screen and I hesitated.

If I answered, I'd likely be greeted by a damn robo call or sales pitch.

But, on the off chance it was someone who wanted to set up an appointment and had somehow gotten my personal number rather than business number, I thumbed the green answer button.

"Cravin' Ink Designs," I said.

"Is this Jett? Jett Nelson?"

An immediate sense of dread traveled through me, making the hair on the back of my head stand up. "Yes?"

"This is Midtown Community Hospital. Is Allen Nelson your grandfather?"

My brain was still stuck on *hospital*, but I did my best to focus. "Yes. What's happened? Is he okay?"

"There was an accident. A friend brought him in, but neither of them have their phones with them and couldn't remember your number. Your grandfather's friend asked me to call you to let you know Allen's being admitted for surgery and observation."

"Surgery? What happened?" My gut roiled with worry.

"Would you be able to come to the hospital, Mr. Nelson?"

"Yes, of course. Can you just let me know he's okay?" I checked the front door was locked, flipped off the lights, and rushed out the back door.

"All I can tell you is he's heading into surgery. Depending on when you arrive, he may or may not be in his room for observation. The doctors will be able to tell you more."

I bit back a scared, frustrated growl. "Okay, I'm on my way."

When I reached the sidewalk, shoving my hand into my pocket to search for my keys out of habit, panicked dismay washed over me.

I had no vehicle here on Cravenwood Block.

Had no need.

Any time Leighton and I had gone farther than walking distance, we'd just ordered an Uber or Lyft.

Fumbling with my phone, I swiped the screen and frantically flipped through the apps.

Fuck.

I'd deleted the app I needed after my credit card had a strange charge. Of course, I'd taken care of it with the card company, but I hadn't yet taken the time to set up the app again because Leighton had just used his app whenever needed.

Leighton.

I rushed toward Cravin'-a-Cup and burst through the door.

Several of the regulars and Leighton's co-workers said hello, but shock and concern registered on their faces the moment they noticed my face.

"Jett?" Leighton asked from behind the counter. "What's wrong?"

"The hospital called. Grandpa had an accident. He's having surgery. Milton—hell, I guess it was Milton—took him. I need to get there, but I don't have a car. Can I use your app?" The words rushed out of me in a whoosh.

Leighton had his apron off and his phone out within moments as he walked toward me. "Come on, we'll wait out front. There's a car available three minutes away."

"Thanks, you don't have to go." My chest constricted. I wanted him to go. I didn't want to be there on my own. Didn't want to be alone with my thoughts on the drive.

Leighton turned and cupped my face with his delicate fingers. "Do you not want me with you?"

"I want you there," I strangled out.

"Then I'm there. Work is fine, I was almost off shift

anyway. We'll get there and find out what's going on. Grandpa will be happy to see you."

Our ride pulled up and we climbed inside.

Luckily, the drive to Midtown Community Hospital was only about thirty minutes, but it gave me way too much time to imagine the absolute worst.

I appreciated Leighton's hand in mine, his solid presence, his ability to calm me with just a soft caress of his thumb.

"What if..." I started, the words and thoughts too much for me to keep going. Grandpa was my parent in every way that truly counted. He was the only friend I'd had for a very long time. I knew I'd lose him one day, but I wasn't ready for it to be so soon. He wasn't *old* and I'd always thought he still had plenty of life left in him.

"Let's not borrow trouble," Leighton soothed. "We'll get there and hear what the doctors have to say. Talk to Milton. No need to build up the worst in our heads until we have information."

I leaned into him. "Thanks. Just sucks that there's about a million possibilities and I'm imagining the worst of the worst."

"I know. It's hard. Just try to hold off until we get details."

The driver dropped us at the door and I rushed to the desk, immediately registering the sterile scent and cold air. Why did hospitals have to automatically feel so negative even when almost everyone there was doing their best to save lives?

Thanks to Leighton, we found the floor Grandpa would be staying on while he recovered. Milton rose from his chair in the waiting room and rushed to us, hugging first me and then Leighton.

"Allen will be so glad you're here. They came out and updated me a bit ago. The surgery went as expected and he'll be in his room shortly. I told them you were on your way. He can have two visitors at a time, so you two can go back when he's ready."

"What happened? What was the surgery for?" Heart attack and stroke were running through my head, but I thought I recalled the lady on the phone mentioning an accident.

Milton gestured to the little couch and we sat, Leighton wrapping his arm through mine and pulling his legs up under him. If Milton noticed or thought anything of it, he didn't indicate.

Grandpa's friend smiled. "Well, Allen probably would rather I not tell you, but he was using a chainsaw to clear some trees on his property. Something slipped and the chainsaw cut his leg. Bled a lot and the doctors had to do the surgery to go in and cauterize some of the blood vessels and clean up the mess he made of the bone. They said it wasn't a good accident to have, but it could have been much worse. He's all patched up now."

"Fuck," I breathed out in a rush. Okay, so that scenario hadn't even crossed my mind. "So, he's going to be okay?"

Milton nodded. "Doctors can answer more of your questions, but they expect him to make a full recovery."

At that moment, the doors to the waiting room opened and a smiling nurse walked out. "With Allen Nelson?"

I stood, pulling Leighton up with me. "I'm his grandson."

"He's expecting you. He can have two visitors, but not for long." She glanced to where Leighton was still clutching my hand. "This way."

Grandpa smiled happily—maybe still from the drugs—when Leighton and I walked in. He was groggy and embarrassed that he'd had such a silly mishap—his words, not mine—but he told us what had happened and how Milton had rushed over.

"I called to see if he had some bandages, but he convinced me I needed to be seen by professionals. Figured they'd just stitch me up, wasn't expecting emergency surgery. Docs said if the saw had gone any deeper, I would have been in a lot more danger of bleeding out or tearing my leg up in a way that couldn't be so easily repaired."

"Shit," I muttered. "No more chainsaws. We'll hire people for that from now on."

"As bad as this damn leg is throbbing, I'm not even gonna argue with you on that." Grandpa laughed.

The three of us spent thirty minutes chatting before the nurse came to usher us out.

"I'll be back in your room as soon as visiting hours start tomorrow," I told Grandpa with a hand on his shoulder.

Milton agreed to go home to clean up and rest. He'd bring clothes for Grandpa when he returned.

Leighton hugged me close in an empty hallway and pulled me down for a kiss. "I'll be back tomorrow after my shift. Are you sure you want to sleep in the waiting room?"

"No worries, I'm sure they'll give me a pillow and

blanket. Just wanna be here in case something happens. Wanna talk to the doctor first thing and see what his recovery is going to look like." I hugged him, kissing him deeply. "Thanks for bringing me and being here for me."

Leighton grinned and winked with a shrug. "That's what friends are for, right?"

He might as well have kneed me in the nuts, but I smiled and nodded. "Yeah. Right. Thanks." I walked him down to where his Uber was waiting. "I'll talk to you tomorrow," I whispered against his ear.

Returning upstairs, I asked the kind nurses if I'd be able to borrow a pillow and blanket and camp out in the waiting room. It wasn't the most comfortable sleeping arrangement, but I felt better knowing I was there in case anything unexpected happened with Grandpa. I mean, he'd already surprised the shit out of me by slicing his leg open with a chainsaw, who knew what else might happen.

The alarm on my phone woke me in time to stretch my stiff joints and make my way to the bathroom the next morning. I splashed water on my face and rinsed my mouth in hopes of washing away the worst of the morning breath.

By the time I'd taken a piss and run a hand through my hair, deciding I was as put together as I was gonna get, I plastered on a smile and approached the nurse station. "Can I see Allen Nelson?"

"Of course. Visiting hours are seven to eleven and again one to four. He can have two visitors at a time, but we ask that you let him rest." The older woman waved me toward the door that led to Grandpa's room.

"Thanks."

Grandpa and I spent the first two hours chatting with friendly nurses as they popped in to check vitals and administer medication. Grandpa's breakfast wasn't terrible according to him, but the coffee we split was definitely not from Cravin'-a-Cup.

"Well, how's the patient doing?" a thin, wiry man with glasses and a comb-over asked as he walked in studying a tablet.

"Ready to bust this joint, Doc," Grandpa said with a laugh.

"I think that's going to be possible. We'll get you up and walking today. If that goes well, we'll get the paperwork ready. You may be able to head home by later this afternoon." The doctor glanced between Grandpa and me. "Now, a few things before we make that happen. Stairs are completely out for six weeks. And you're going to need someone there to take care of you."

My heart plummeted, but I knew there was no way I could send Grandpa home by himself, even if the doctor hadn't demanded it.

"He'll have someone. No worries," I piped up, ignoring the look Grandpa gave me.

"Now, it's not going to be a twenty-four-seven issue, just someone to make sure he takes it easy, stays off the stairs, gets his medicine, that kind of thing. We'll make sure you know how to change your bandages. You'll follow up with your primary in a week and then however often they want to see you." The doctor tapped away on the tablet. "You're lucky, Mr. Nelson. That could have been much worse. No more chainsaws for a while, huh?"

"My chainsaw days are over, Doc."

Grandpa and I napped for a while after the doctor's visit.

When a nurse came in at the end of morning visiting hours, she winked. "If the two of you promise to keep quiet and rest, you can stay."

I gratefully accepted the extra time with Grandpa even though it gave me way too much time to think about the fact I was going to have to move back to his house. Not that I wasn't completely willing to do whatever it took to get Grandpa healed up and back on his feet, I just wasn't looking forward to the change.

To leaving Leighton.

A bit later, one of the nurses came in to take Grandpa on a walk. "I'll be back later, okay?" I asked and Grandpa gave me an enthusiastic wave as he set off down the hall with his IV pole and the nurse.

As I headed downstairs in search of a toothbrush and food, my phone buzzed.

Leighton.

He was getting out of an Uber and heading inside.

I replied that he should meet me in the giftshop because I desperately needed a toothbrush.

My sunshiny hurricane met me with a smile in front of the giftshop. "No need to shop. I brought you toothbrush, toothpaste, deodorant, and new clothes." He handed me a duffle bag.

"You are the best." I hugged him close. "Give me five minutes in the bathroom and we can go eat."

"Got that covered, too." He held up a Cravin'-a-Cup box which I knew held food and *good* coffee.

"God, I love you so hard right now," I said, pressing a kiss to his cheek before realizing what I'd said.

I did.

Love him.

But things were going to have to change.

Plus, Leighton didn't want that.

So, I chuckled and held up my duffle. "You're a lifesaver."

Leighton's bright eyes sparkled. "Least I could do. Figured you'd had a long night. I'll meet you over there in that sitting area."

Five minutes later, feeling human again, I sat down next to Leighton on the loveseat and did my best not to scarf down every last bite of food in thirty seconds flat.

"So, how's Grandpa?" Leighton asked, sipping his drink.

"May get to go home today."

"Wow, already? That's great." Leighton cocked his head. "What's wrong? Why don't you seem happy?"

"No, I'm happy. But…" I paused and smiled, gratefully accepting the toothpick Leighton held out for me. Rolling it between my lips and biting down on it, I took a moment to think about what I had to say before I continued. "I think I'm going to need to move back to Grandpa's for about six to eight weeks."

Leighton's brows shot up and I swore he looked devastated.

Part of that reaction had me feeling hopeful.

But if I was moving out for two months, how would our friends-with-benefits continue? It wasn't like I could expect him to just put his life on hold for me.

"Grandpa can't live on his own during recovery. Doctor said he has to have help. I don't want to move out, but I'm the logical choice. My parents sure as hell won't go help—and, even though they could afford to hire someone for him, they won't...not that he'd accept the help from them anyway—so it looks like I'll be living with him again for a while."

Leighton took my hand. "I don't want to lose my best friend for two months, but I understand why you have to do it. It's only two months, I promise to not sublet your room. At least not until the third month," he teased.

"Do you think I should just see about getting out of my lease and moving back to Grandpa's permanently?" I wondered aloud.

"What?" Leighton looked stricken. "Absolutely not, snookie."

"Call me that again and I'll go straight to Julian tonight," I said, nudging his shoulder.

"Fine, fine. But, *no*, I do *not* think you should get out of your lease. Two months is nothing. Keep the lease, stay with Grandpa, come back when he's doing fine on his own. Moving out permanently wouldn't make sense." Leighton glanced up at me. "Unless you don't want to be there?"

"That's not it at all. Just feeling a little selfish right now. Like, I know I have to be the one to step up and help him—hell, he took care of me all those years—but I'm being greedy because I don't want to give up what I've got on Cravenwood Block."

Leighton placed a hand on my thigh. "No giving up necessary. Just a little pause."

I wondered briefly if he was talking about my apartment situation or what he and I had going on.

When we made our way back up to Grandpa's floor, we found him and Milton laughing over something on the television. My eyes immediately zoned in on Milton's hand holding Grandpa's.

Huh.

That was...

Different?

New?

Unexpected?

But I knew all about different, new, and unexpected friendships and how they could seep into every cell in your body.

I did my best to clear the...I wasn't even sure what it was. Not shock or confusion, maybe just the stretching of my brain as it wrapped around the new development. Milton and Grandpa were close friends. Beyond that, it wasn't my business and I was happy they had each other.

"Milton, can you and Leighton give me and Jett a little time?" Grandpa asked and Milton nodded.

"Of course. I'll see about sneaking in some decent coffee later."

Leighton and Grandpa exchanged pleasantries before Milton and Leighton left the room.

"Sorry, didn't know Milton was here. Didn't mean to interrupt," I said, taking the vacated seat.

"No worries, if it means he can bring me decent coffee, it's worth it." Grandpa took my hand. "I wanted to talk to you about going home."

"It's all good. I've got it planned. I'll keep the

apartment for the time being and move back in with you..."

Grandpa held up a hand to stop me. "That's not necessary."

My brows shot up. "Excuse me? Yes, it is. You heard the doctor. You need someone with you while you recover."

"I'm selling my house and moving in with Milton."

I blinked. "What? That seems a bit drastic."

"Don't be dramatic. It's not drastic. I've been thinking of selling for a while. Milton has the room. I'll recover just fine at his place and I'll be happy to be rid of the property upkeep on my place."

"Or, you could just let your grandson take care of you the way you took care of him for all those years." My heart was torn between wanting to be a good grandson and care for Grandpa and being thrilled to think I wouldn't have to leave my friends and Leighton.

"I *could*, but that would mean taking him away from his new home, his business, and his someone special. No need for that when I can stay with Milton." Grandpa's eyes twinkled.

"You and Milton, huh?" I asked with a smirk, ignoring his *someone special* comment for the moment.

"You and Leighton, huh?" Grandpa retorted.

I shrugged. "Yeah, but it's just a casual thing. He doesn't want more."

"Bullshit, that boy is in love with you. Don't let stupid pride or lack of communication get between you. I like that kid, he's good for you."

"So, you're okay with me being..." I gestured vaguely

toward the direction Leighton had exited. "Being with Leighton?"

"I'm okay with you being happy." Grandpa squeezed my hand. "And if it gives your parents conniption fits, all the better. We should introduce them to Milton and Leighton at a dinner one evening. Personally, I'd love to see their faces."

I laughed. "You're bad, but I like it." Cocking a brow, I repeated. "So, you and Milton?"

"We're good together. Been friends for a long time. Thought that's all it was...that *was* all it was for the longest time...but we've realized it's a bit more. He was lonely for a long time after his wife died. I've been on my own since your grandmother moved on from our lackluster marriage. We're a good fit."

"Do you love him?" I asked.

"I do. We have something special. It wouldn't work for everyone, but it works for us." Grandpa shifted, wincing at what I assumed was pain in his leg. "Do you love Leighton?"

I swallowed thickly and nodded.

"Then tell him. He deserves to know and you can't build a loving relationship without talking—the good, the bad, and the ugly," Grandpa said.

"It's not that easy. When I first realized I had a thing for him, we agreed to completely casual, nothing more. He's been hurt in the past. If I tell him I love him and want something more, I risk losing what we have going on *and* the friendship."

Grandpa grunted. "Nonsense. If he'd give up what you have just because you love him, he's not the man I think he is. Ever think that maybe he's worried to tell you how he really feels because he thinks *you* just want casual? Talk. To. Him." He yawned. "Now, get on out of here and send Milton back in. We've got shows to watch. I'll let you know once I'm home."

"Damn, old man. Anyone ever tell you you're bossy?" I leaned down and gave him a hug. "Let me know if you need anything."

"Will do. Thanks for being here. Let's plan that dinner with your parents," he said with an evil gleam in his eyes.

I found Milton and Leighton in the waiting room. "He wants you back in there to watch shows."

Milton smiled and stood up.

"We're going to head out," I said. "You'll let me know if either of you need *anything*?"

He nodded. "Of course. He'll be comfortable at my place. Promise."

"Take care of him," I croaked, suddenly exhausted and overwhelmed. "I'm glad he's got you."

"Will do," Milton said. "He's in good hands. And I'm glad *I've* got *him*."

Milton walked through the doors to Grandpa's room.

"Ready?" I held out my hand to Leighton.

"What was that?" he asked.

"Seems Grandpa and Milton have a *thing* going on. He's selling his place and moving in with Milton. So, I don't need to move in with him during his recovery. In fact, he pretty much forbade it." The whole situation seemed unreal.

"What? Really? Whoa," Leighton mused. "That's

crazy, but I can see it. So, I don't get to sublet your room?"

I put him in a headlock. "No. But you can get me home before I fall asleep standing up."

"You truly don't look so great." Leighton took my hand and led me to the elevator.

"Don't feel so great."

By the time Leighton got me home, my head was throbbing and my limbs were concrete slabs.

"Okay, you need sleep. Lots of sleep. Drink this bottle of water first. I'm going to get you something for your head while you shower." Leighton stripped me and all but shoved me into the hot shower.

When he returned a bit later, I hadn't moved from under the stream of water.

"Wash yourself and get out," Leighton pressed. "I've got medicine and Gatorade. You can sleep for twelve hours if needed."

In a fog, I washed, dried, and climbed into bed. "Sleep with me," I mumbled after taking the pills and swigging the Gatorade.

"I will, but I'm going to grab drinks and snacks, let the guys know what's up, make sure we have chargers first; I'll be back." He pressed a kiss to my lips. "Sleep, babe."

I was already asleep before I could argue the nickname. I guess it wasn't the *worst*.

I slept hard for the next twelve hours.

I'd wake to find the bed empty and feel alone, wishing Leighton was with me.

I'd wake to find Leighton curled in my arms and feel complete, like the world was right.

When I finally woke for good, pulled from slumber by Leighton's off-key singing and cute, sexy dancing as he gathered up trash and bottles from my bedside table, I couldn't help the smile that filled my face.

"He sings, dances, *and* cleans? Love it." I reached for him.

Leighton tossed all the trash in a big bag and toppled on top of me. "Sorry to wake you, but I figured you needed to get up so you can get your sleep schedule somewhat back on track. How do you feel?"

"'Bout to piss my pants, but I'm feeling a lot better." I smacked a kiss to his lips and rolled from bed to rush to the bathroom.

When I returned, running a hand through my messy hair, I thought back on the happenings of the last couple days. "Did my grandpa really tear up his leg with a chainsaw, have to have surgery, let me offer to move back in with him, tell me he and Milton have something going on, and opt to sell his house and move in with his lover?"

Leighton snorted. "Yes. All of that happened."

"Damn. No wonder I was exhausted." I looked at the time on my phone. "Wanna go grab dinner and see what the guys are doing? I need to stay busy if I'm going to sleep tonight."

"Sounds perfect. We desperately need groceries, you up for a trip to the store at some point?"

"That will definitely wear me out," I teased. "Dinner first. Maybe drinks if Lucas is working?"

"Let's go." Leighton glanced down at his shorts and t-shirt. "And by *let's go*, I mean give me at least an hour to get ready."

I laughed. "Wouldn't have expected anything less."

By the time we headed out for dinner, that calm contented feeling was wrapped around me again.

"I'm really glad your grandpa is okay," Leighton said as we made our way down the stairs.

"Me, too."

"And I'm really glad you don't have to move in with him. I knew why you needed to and I would have supported you through it, but I'm glad you're still here, roomie."

I swallowed against an unexpected emotion and put my arm around his shoulder. "Me, too. It was the right thing to do, but that didn't make it easy."

Feeling grateful and happy—doing my best to avoid the confusing mess of thoughts regarding where the thing between Leighton and me could go—I kept him tucked under my arm and took my guy out for dinner and drinks.

TWELVE

Leighton

WOULD BEST-FRIENDS-WITH-BENEFITS have such easy and fun date nights?

I wanted to think *no*.

But Jett and I always had fun together. Coffee and a walk in the Cravenwood park, dinner and drinks, a movie and shopping at the great little shops on Cravenwood Block.

It didn't matter what we were doing, we had fun.

Was that because we were friends first and foremost?

Or because we had something special?

If the sex stopped, would we still have fun?

Yes.

I knew without a doubt.

So, was the sex just a bonus to our relationship? Something I needed to learn to live without?

I'd do it.

If it meant keeping Jett in my life.

No question, I'd do it in a heartbeat.

But the deepest fathoms of my soul said we had

something more than just friendship, something more than just easy, fun sex.

And after our date the night before, I was determined to be upfront and honest. I *had* to talk to Jett—let him know how I was feeling. I was convinced we wouldn't lose the friendship, even if things got a little bumpy, but I owed it to the two of us to acknowledge how my feelings had changed and see if we could get ourselves on the same page.

Our dinner the night before had turned out to be bar food at Cravenwood Tap—Jett smiling proudly and nudging my shoulder when I ordered my fish without lettuce and tomato, add cheese and pickle, and tartar sauce on the side.

We spent a couple hours laughing over fun drinks that Lucas just kept sliding in front of us. He claimed we were great test subjects to try his newest concoctions on a slow night.

Groceries got pushed aside when Jett and I were too buzzed to even consider heading to the store.

Sex with Jett was always good—I loved the two sides of him during sex. Side one was the Jett who used to just endure sex now absolutely loving every single thing about it. Side two was Jett learning about himself and what he enjoyed, experimenting with a trusted friend, and getting bolder about asking for what he wanted.

The night before, he'd begged me to finger him while sucking him off. When he'd recovered, he fucked me to within an inch of my life, his wide frame spread out over me as he pressed me into the mattress, his cock thrusting hard and fast until I made a mess of my bed.

That was how we ended up in his bed, my sheets being washed, as we did our best to avoid a trip to the grocery store the next afternoon.

But we'd finally pulled ourselves from our cozy cocoon and made our way to the market.

We made a great team when it came to grocery shopping. Ollie and I weren't allowed to go on our own because we ended up with a bunch of junk. Julian and Shaw were a decent team. Ollie swore Bash was boring in the store. Lucas and Dean basically shared the same brain so they did a decent job with shopping together. But I truly thought Jett and I did the best—not only did we get the job done, made it a game to save as much money as possible, we had fun and usually came home with something new to try.

"Glad that's over," Jett said as he pulled the wagon onto the elevator, both of us carrying a few reusable bags that wouldn't fit into the wagon. "Wanna try that orange chicken and rice tonight? I like the other brand, but maybe this one will be even better."

His words were nothing special, but as I watched him pull the wagon out of the elevator and make his way toward our apartment door, a wash of emotions flooded over me.

Images of us five, ten, twenty years down the road.

But only if I grabbed life by the balls and owned up to my feelings for him.

If I kept how I was feeling a secret, someone was eventually going to take Jett away from me. Yes, I knew he was likely demisexual and that meant he'd have to build a closeness with that person first, but it wasn't out of the question.

If I kept letting him believe I didn't want anything more than casual, he'd eventually find someone else.

Or maybe he wouldn't, but how long could I keep pretending that what we had wasn't real—at least on my side of things.

Yeah, maybe I'd spill my guts and he'd balk.

Maybe he was counting on nothing between us being real.

But in all honesty, that was a bunch of bullshit.

Our friendship was the most real thing I'd ever experienced.

Sure, we'd started sex as just easy and fun, but I'd never had such a strong connection to any sexual partner, and I credited that to the strength of our friendship.

So, all my worries about wanting something *real* with Jett were unfounded. We already had the realest of real.

I just needed him to know it wasn't just fun and casual for me anymore.

It was *fun* for sure. But I'd gone and fallen in love with him and I needed him to know that.

Jett unloaded the wagon, folding and storing it in the hall closet, and returned to emptying bags in the kitchen.

"I'm sorry," I blurted. "I tried, but I just can't do it. Can't keep doing this."

Jett turned wide, sad eyes my way, and took a deep breath. "It's okay." He lifted his chin, gnawing on his toothpick, jaw tight. "I knew where you stood from the beginning. We both knew this wasn't going to last."

My stomach plummeted.

"What? No, babe, I'm saying I'm sorry because I let you get into this thing thinking I didn't want anything serious—and I really tried to keep it casual—but I've been in love with you probably since the first day I waltzed into your shop." I took his hands in mine, trying to fight it, but grinning like a damn lunatic. "Nothing feels right when you're not around. I'll understand if you don't want something more serious with me, but I can't keep lying about my feelings for you."

Jett gripped my hands and pushed me against the counter. "Are you for real right now?"

"Um, yes?"

"Fuck, Leigh, you can't just drop this shit on me." He pressed his forehead against mine. "You love me? Like for real? This isn't just me taking advantage of a situation? Using your past to get to you?"

I shook my head, determined to make him understand. "Not at all. Stephon *used me*, you didn't. Not even close."

"But I kinda did. I took the casual sex offered because I was desperate to be with you." Jett dipped his head, looking sheepish. "I've wanted something more with you since we started this whole thing, but I thought casual was all you wanted. I feel like I used you just like he did."

"Well," I chuckled, "we've been on the same page since the beginning because I only offered casual because I thought it was the only way you'd take me up on it."

"So, you don't think I took advantage?"

"Did you ever once pretend I was someone else? Imagine me being a girl? Fuck me and then leave my bed to go to your girlfriend?"

"Fuck, no. You know I didn't," Jett growled. "Never."

"Then we're all good." I cupped my hands around his face and leaned up on tiptoes to kiss him. "I'm hopelessly in love with you. I get it if you need time to process—"

"I love you," Jett rushed out. "I think I've loved you since the first day Hurricane Leighton blew into my shop."

I cocked a brow.

Jett shrugged. "It's how I've always thought of you, my little sunshiny hurricane."

"That's possibly the sappiest, most romantic thing I've ever heard. I love it."

"So, I've got a plethora of nicknames for you... Hurricane, Cane, Storm, Sunshine...and you've still not settled on one for me," Jett murmured against my lips.

"Honestly? I don't even care about the nickname, as long as I can call you mine." I opened my mouth for him, welcoming his warm, slick tongue as he claimed me.

"How about *babe* when you feel the need? And being called *yours* is perfect." Jett reclaimed my mouth, rocking his hips into mine.

"I can't believe you love me," I said, my heart nearly beating out of my chest, the warmth of perfection and promise washing over me.

"Believe it," Jett said. "We were a couple dumbasses for way too long, but I'm never letting you go. You said you love me and I'm holding you to that." He sighed and tucked my head under his chin. "Fuck, I love you."

"Holy shit," Ollie exclaimed from the doorway. "Did you two finally pull your heads from your asses and admit you're in love? Damn, took you long enough. I'll warn Julian and Shaw to put in earplugs; thank god we don't share a wall with you."

Jett flipped Ollie off and ushered me to our apartment.

"Shower, prep, whatever. Please tell me you have a late shift tomorrow," Jett growled at my ear. "Because I plan to keep you in bed until then."

"I definitely have a late shift, and I'd call off if I didn't."

We each took some time to ourselves in the bathroom and I trembled slightly when I walked into Jett's room to see Gatorade, protein drinks, protein bars, and water.

Jett shrugged and winked. "Figured we'd need to refuel. Now, get in bed."

————

"OH MY GOD, LEIGH," Jett gasped after I'd ridden him to his second orgasm in just under two hours. "Are you trying to fit every sexual act and position into the hours before we go to work?"

"Of course not," I quipped, biting his neck as his spent cock slid from my well-used ass. "I probably only know like half of them anyway. So, maybe trying to fit in half of that half?" A laugh rumbled through me when Jett groaned. "I'll let you rest. You're no good to me if you're broken."

We slept for an unknown amount of time, but it was still dark when I cracked my eye open and looked toward Jett's window.

"Would you ever want to fuck me?" Jett asked, his voice clear enough I could tell he'd been awake for a while. "I mean, I'm not even sure I'd like it, but if I wanted to try—"

"Yes, fucking hell, yes." I fought the urge to squeal as I

pulled him on top of me, spreading my legs to make room for his.

Jett chuckled. "Will you be upset if I don't like it?"

"No, babe. Don't be silly. I mostly just keep you around for a slick pole to service my greedy little homo hole—"

He snorted very ungracefully and kissed me, but that only shut me up for so long.

"As I was saying, I'm mostly a slut for dick, and I doubt that will ever change. But, from time to time, a girl likes to put her cock to good use, and there's no ass I'd rather plow than yours, sweet pea."

"No," Jett growled. "And not now, you've got to give me at least a little instruction on prepping beyond a thorough, in-depth scrubbing, but I wanna try."

"I promise to introduce you to the ins and outs—quite literally—of douching. Consider it Prep 101. I'm a master teacher and you will excel in all aspects of the class." I burst out laughing when Jett tickled my torso.

"Do you ever shut up?"

"I've heard old wives tales that shoving a dick in my ass is sometimes successful in getting me to stop talking. It may be worth a shot." I squirmed under his broad body, whimpering when our rock-hard cocks rubbed together, Jett's fiery eyes locked with mine.

"I wanna fuck you just like this, wanna watch my cock sliding in and out of that pretty hole," Jett said, kissing my neck, biting hard enough I knew there'd be a mark.

I rocked my hips. "Your wish is my command, just get in me already," I begged.

"I don't know how your ass isn't sore yet." Jett grabbed for the lube.

"Oh, don't get me wrong, I'm sore, but it's the type of hurt that hurts so good." I took the bottle from him. "Go sparingly, I'm still slick from your last load."

"Jesus, Leigh, keep saying shit like that and I'll fucking nut right here."

I laughed. "Do you have anything left to nut?"

Jett grabbed me by the shoulders and pressed his cock into me. "Guess you're gonna find out, huh? Think that greedy little hole can milk anything else from me?"

Turned out, my greedy little hole definitely came through.

Later, as Jett held me and we pretended we didn't have to get out of bed soon to go face the rest of our day, he reached over his head and knocked three times on the wall.

My heart soared. As my eyes locked with his, I shifted to return the three knocks.

Jett gave a wicked grin and shrugged. "Eh, I'm fine."

"You ass," I exclaimed. "You know I meant I love—"

"And I love you, too." He pressed his lips against my temple. "Who would have guessed I'd find my happily ever after on Cravenwood Block?"

I popped up on an elbow and grinned down at him. "I mean, *cravin' wood* and happily ever after? They're kinda the same thing."

Jett laughed and slapped my ass. "You ever gonna get that new tattoo?"

I rolled from bed and shrugged, propping a hand on my naked hip and stroking fingers over the bare skin where I wanted the ink. "I don't know. I've kinda got a thing for the tattoo artist. Maybe he'll let me get under his gun soon."

Jett yanked me back onto the bed, growling about getting me under his gun.

We were both very late for work.

Bonus Scene #1

JETT

"You doing okay?" Leighton asked from the other side of the door as I stood in the shower following his directions for the douche.

"Yeah, I'm good. I'm on the last step." Holding it in was a lot harder than I'd anticipated, but I'd moved from the toilet when things were running clear and stepped into the shower for the last round. With my insides quivering and thighs trembling, I turned on the shower. Stepping under the warm stream, I did as Leighton had instructed.

He'd offered to be by my side during the process, but I'd assured him his directions had been very detailed. Although, not gonna lie, I *could* see how the whole process, if shared with the right person, could kinda be erotic.

I washed, rinsed, and washed again before stepping out and drying off.

Leighton and I had *officially* been together three

months, which put us knowing each other right around six months, and things had never been better.

I'd wanted to bottom for him right away, but between visits to Grandpa as he recovered, and our work schedules getting totally outta whack again, we truly hadn't had much time for trying anything new.

Don't get me wrong, we stayed plenty busy and satisfied in bed.

Truly, take away the sex, and I'd still be just as happy and satisfied with my little sunshiny hurricane.

But the sex was awesome.

Leighton had insisted on using a dildo on my ass as he sucked me off every night the past week. "I need you properly stretched when I get this monster cock in your hole," he'd deadpanned.

I'd taken advantage of his self-deprecation to assure him I was highly satisfied with his cock size. Then I'd shown him with my mouth just how perfectly-sized he was for me. He wasn't super wide, but like his long, slim fingers, I knew he'd have no problem hitting my prostate.

Fuck.

I was already hard and leaking under the towel.

"Okay, get on the bed," Leighton warned. "I've gotta be honest, this likely won't last long. I've been edging myself in the shower the last week, but every time I imagine my cock in your ass, I blow my load like a fourteen-year-old."

I stretched out on the bed and stroked my shaft. "No problem. You fill my ass and I'll fill your mouth."

"Fuck, bunny, that's so damn hot." Leighton knelt and

pushed my legs apart, licking over my taint and then my hole.

I shivered, not even bothering to nix the nickname.

I'd purposely not jacked off since we'd figured out a time for me to try bottoming, so I was strung tight and ready to blow.

"Fuck, Leigh, get the lube and get in me," I begged, gripping my cock hard.

"Damn, I've taught you well." Leighton pretended to wipe tears. "My eager pupil has become the bossy bottom I've always known he could be." He reached for the lube and slicked himself before smearing my hole.

Not gonna lie, the dildos and Leighton sucking me off had been fun and I wasn't against doing that from time to time. But I really wanted to feel Leighton in me. I had a feeling we'd default to me topping more often than not, and I was completely on board with that, but knowing how badly Leighton wanted to fuck me was a total turn on.

"Ready?" Leighton asked, his cock head pressed against my pucker. "Relax and push against me a little."

The dildos had been good.

Leighton was better.

The smooth heat of his skin sliding in and out of me set me on fire. The pull of his flared cock head as he pulled almost out of me, the zap of electricity jolting through me when his long dick brushed over that sensitive bundle of nerves.

"Fuck," I bit out, stroking my cock.

"Damn, baby, you feel so fucking good," Leighton gritted out, pressing my knees open wider, and cupping my balls, lifting them up so he could see where he entered me. "Fuck, Jett, not gonna last. Jack yourself. Come for me, wanna feel this pretty ass come on my cock."

Leighton's dirty talk made me laugh when we were joking around, but in bed turned my blood to lava. I gripped my cock and stroked, feeling the tingle in my lower back as my balls drew up tight.

"Kiss me," I demanded, loving the way Leighton immediately dropped between my spread legs to devour my mouth. "Fuck, Leigh, I'm close."

He moved back to watch me jerk my dick, groaning as I exploded in long thick ropes of cum on my stomach and chest, my ass clenching around his thrusting cock. "Come for me, Leigh. Wanna feel your cum dripping from my ass."

"Fuuuuck," Leighton moaned, his fingers digging into my thighs as he slammed into me over and over. With a final thrust, his cock shot his hot load deep into me, pulsing his release, my tight ring of muscles milking every last drop from him.

"Jesus," I groaned, wincing as Leighton pulled gently from my body.

"I mean, I know that was good, but I'm not the son of god," Leighton quipped, falling onto me and cuddling close when I wrapped him in my arms and rolled us to the side.

"We need to work on your humbleness," I deadpanned.

"Jetty—"

"God, no."

"Jetters?"

"Fuck off."

Leighton sighed. "Baby, there's not a humble bone in my fabulous body and you love me anyway."

"There's going to be a bone in your body if you give me about thirty minutes," I growled against his ear. "And yeah, I love you just the way you are."

Bonus Scene #2

LEIGHTON

"Any particular reason you had me come in for my tattoo after hours?" I asked when Jett closed the door and flipped the sign to *Closed*.

Not gonna lie, I was a bit more nervous about the original design he was inking on my *low* lower abdomen. Getting the one on my ass had burned, but I wouldn't have called it painful. The one I was getting now—low enough we'd be entering pube territory if I didn't already keep things nice and neat down there—was in a more sensitive spot.

Jett wrapped me in his arms and dipped his head for a long, slow kiss. I always loved how he kissed me when we'd been apart—no matter how long we hadn't seen each other, he kissed me as if he'd been missing me for years.

"Save my open hours for paying customers," he murmured against my lips.

"Hey!" I swatted at him. "I offered to pay and you said my cash wasn't needed."

"Don't want your money." He cupped my face and

pressed his forehead to mine, breathing me in with a groan. "Maybe we make payment plans of a different sort."

"Mmmm, sounds nasty, I like it. Whatdya have in mind?"

"My office. Now." Jett spun me around and maneuvered me toward the backroom where he kept a desk, a small fridge, a microwave, and a shelf full of his drawing supplies. "Strip."

I gladly lost all my clothing, my eager cock plumping in anticipation of whatever Jett had in mind.

We lost ourselves in long, slow kisses and unhurried strokes and caresses.

Jett pushed me against the desk and dropped to his knees, taking me deep into his mouth as he worshiped my cock and stretched my hole with spit-slick fingers.

"Stop," I gasped when my balls drew up tight, ready to burst. "Don't wanna come yet. You're very overdressed for this," I teased.

Jett shucked his clothes off and pulled me close, our warm, naked skin coming together in a burst of sensation that took my breath away.

Pushing him to take a seat in his desk chair, I knelt between his spread legs and fondled his balls before swirling my tongue around his leaking head. "You have any lube?" Spit would do, but lube was easier.

"Vaseline," Jett grunted and gestured toward an unopened tub on the shelf.

"Gotta love a man who can improvise," I joked, grateful for his need to use the substance in his tattooing. I grabbed the tub and smeared my hole before coating him. "Messy," I laughed, reaching for a paper towel to clean the thick greasiness from my hand.

"Fuck, Leigh, get over here," Jett demanded.

"Shift down," I directed, straddling him and situating myself in a viable position. "Get that pretty cock in me."

Working around the somewhat awkward position in the chair, we shifted ourselves until Jett's cockhead was pressed against my hole. I lowered myself down his shaft, my body rejoicing with each glorious inch he gave me.

I bottomed out and paused, wrapping my arms around his neck and staring into those gorgeous dark eyes. Just when I thought we were heading for a quick, nasty fuck, the vibe between us changed to something more serious, slow and emotional—like the connection between us had grown ten-fold.

Jett made love to me in that chair—in a weird, uncomfortable position with legs and chair arms and wheels causing issues, but nothing else mattered except the joining of our bodies and souls. He rolled the chair to the wall, bracing himself and pulling me close as he sat up, capturing my cock between our writhing sweaty bodies. His warm strength engulfed me as he whispered gruff words of love in my ear, rocking his hips and bringing me closer and closer to the edge.

"Touch me," I begged. "Make me come."

Jett reached between our bodies and stroked my throbbing cock as he thrust into my ass. "Fuck, Leigh," he growled. "Come for me, wanna feel you come around my cock."

The desperation in his words and the heat between us sent me over the edge. I cried out his name as my release exploded over his fist, my ass clenching around his thick shaft.

Jett joined me a moment later, thrusting his hips up with a grunt as he shot his load deep in my ass.

By the time we came down from our high, I worried my legs weren't going to hold me if I was even able to extricate myself from the chair. We spent several long, glorious moments kissing and basking in the love between us.

Jett moaned. "If we're doing this tattoo today, we better get cleaned up."

"Better do it today. Maybe while I'm high from a good orgasm it won't hurt so bad," I said.

He chuckled. "Maybe. At least it's pretty small, it won't take long."

We cleaned up and Jett swooped into professional mode with his organizing and sanitizing before having me stretch out on the table so he could get the stencil applied.

"Do other guys flop their dick out while you're working?" I asked.

Jett snorted. "No. Usually I keep them as covered as possible—girls too. But since your dick's been in my mouth and ass, I don't think it matters that it's exposed."

"Good point," I agreed.

"Ready?"

I whimpered slightly. "As I'll ever be."

Jett worked quickly and efficiently. The pain was worse than when I had my ass done, but not excruciating. I was so in love with the deep swirls of varied teals, purples, and pinks, I was able to forget the discomfort. I'd told Jett which colors I wanted and asked for something abstract and somewhat fluid in design and he'd delivered perfectly.

"You don't have to wait for me if you wanna go on home," Jett said as he started to clean.

"No way I'm missing a chance to walk home with my hot ass man. I'll wait."

An hour later, we headed out.

"You want coffee?"

"Are you buying?"

"Sure," Jett said, wrapping an arm around my shoulders.

"Does it get any better than this?" I asked, leaning into him.

"Better than your boyfriend buying you coffee?"

"Better than finding your true love and spending nights like this together," I said.

"Living and loving on Cravenwood Block," Jett murmured into the top of my head as we walked into Cravin'-a-Cup.

Bonus Scene #3

JETT

"Damn, that was amazing, sugar lips," Leighton murmured against my neck.

"No."

"What about sugar dick? Better?" he teased. "More like magic dick."

I snorted. "No and no." Wrapping my arms around him, I held onto the moment. "You know, we don't *have* to do this."

"Do what? Go to dinner with your parents where they think it's just you and Grandpa, but you're both bringing the men you're being all homosexual with?"

I couldn't help the groan. "Yeah, that. It's likely to be terrible all around and we don't have to do it."

Leighton sat up. "Do you want your parents to know about us? Know about you?"

I sighed. "Yeah. And I know tonight will be the end of any relationship we might have ever had—which was basically no relationship at all. I'm just worried it's going to get ugly and you or Milton will be hurt."

"Honey bunches, I'm a tough little gay boy. I don't love ugly situations, but I'll make the best of one if you're by my side and it means you get freedom from them." Leighton caressed his hand up and down my torso. "If you'd rather make peace, I can stand by your side for that, too. I just want you to get whatever you need from this dinner. Freedom and closure? Understanding and a chance to start over? You name it, I'm there to work on it with you."

I squeezed his hand before bringing it to my mouth for a kiss.

"The only way they'd ever want to start over is if I was a completely different person and agreed to play their games," I said.

"Well, that's not an option. You're Jett—a gorgeous, smart, successful demisexual with a hot ass twinky boyfriend—and there's no changing any of that. They don't like it, they can kiss my ass." He straddled me and rocked himself against my spent cock. "Speaking of kissing asses, why don't we clean up and you can lick your load from my ass in the shower?"

My raunchy, sexy little hurricane.

We made our way to the shower, still in that stage of our relationship where we wanted to be touching at all times—I wasn't sure if or when that would ever change, and I wasn't sure I wanted it to.

"How do you think Allen and Milton will do tonight?" Leighton asked as he washed my back and pressed his cock against my ass.

"I think they'll be fine. There's been no real

relationship between Grandpa and my dad in the time I've been alive. Grandpa doesn't give a rat's ass and Milton seems to be on the same page. I think, at their ages, and in the situation they're in, they can easily tell most folks to just fuck off." Grandpa and Milton had made the transition from friends to lovers seem as easy as pie, and in a way, I guessed Leighton and I had, too.

Our relationship hadn't just magically appeared. There'd been a lot of work and thought and emotions put into it. We'd both had to deal with our pasts. I'd had to do a lot of soul searching to realize and accept the real me.

If Leighton hadn't come along, I'm not sure I ever would have gotten to the point of figuring myself out. Not that I have it all figured out; neither one of us do. But he is my person and I had no doubt he came into my life at exactly the right time. We maybe both still had some healing and growing to do, but the thought of doing that together didn't seem so scary.

"We don't need them. *You* don't need them." Leighton turned me around and wrapped his slippery arms around me. "Even if this thing between us fizzled—which it won't because we're scorching hot and stupidly sweet together —but still, even if it did, you don't need your parents. You haven't needed them for a long time. They don't deserve you. If they can't accept you as you are, fuck them. You're smart and successful—so what if you like to fuck a certain fine, gay twinky ass?"

"So, you're saying we can say fuck off just as easily?"

"Exactly."

"I just don't want them getting ugly with you or

Grandpa or Milton." I'd been ignoring my parents' shit for most of my life, I didn't want people I loved to have to do the same.

"Baby love, I'm gay, it's almost a prerequisite that I'm down for drama."

I slapped his wet ass and kissed him hard. "Have I told you how happy I am you stalked me until I finally gave in?"

"Almost as much as you've told me how much you love me, but I never get tired of hearing it."

We kissed and caressed, enjoying the warm water and slick skin, until the water cooled.

"Sooo," Leighton tossed my towel to me, "can I be ridiculous tonight?"

"You're ridiculous all the time," I deadpanned as we made our way to my room. His was such a disaster, I preferred we spent most our time in mine—although, when we made a mess of my bed, we often moved to his as backup.

"No, I mean, like over-the-top. If your parents—damn I don't think I even know their names—whatever, if they're rude, can I be the most ridiculous little homo you've ever seen?"

I grabbed him and spun him around, facing us both toward my mirror. The contrast between our skin, hair, eyes, and size never ceased to capture my attention. "Sunshine, I'd pick you and my Grandpa as my *real* family every damn time; you can be as ridiculous as you want." I grabbed his chin and turned his head to kiss him, but pulled back to study his pretty face. "Wait, like what kind of ridiculousness are we talking?"

Leighton huffed. "Well, I'm not going to show them my dildo and plug collection, and I won't go into detail about how good their son eats my ass."

"Oh god. Yeah, let's not get into that."

"I mean, I may insinuate how well their baby boy fucks me with his big ol' cock," Leighton said with a huge grin. "Or we can get real serious and talk about how you recently learned *just* how much you like taking dick or getting *your* ass licked."

"We definitely shouldn't go to dinner."

Leighton pursed his lips. "Why? Am I an embarrassment? You don't want them to know we're in love and fucking like bunnies?"

I chuckled. "Hell, I don't care about that. You can tell them any of that stuff—I'd actually like to see them squirm. I'm just saying all this sexy talk has me wanting to stay home and keep you in bed for a few hours."

"Tell ya what, let's go to dinner. If it gets completely ugly or awkward, we'll head out." He stretched his arms up and back to wrap around my neck, his gorgeous lithe body on full display in the mirror. "But you're welcome to get me off before we leave."

"Such a generous boy," I growled in his ear, sliding my hand down his stomach and taking his hard cock in my fist. "We're going to be late."

Leighton whimpered and thrust his hips. "And I'll happily tell them *why* if they decide to be bitches."

We were *definitely* late, but I didn't give a fuck.

As the Uber pulled up in front of my parents' house, the memory of Leighton's soft moans sounding in my ears as I brought him off fueled me to face whatever the night brought our way.

"We ready for this?" Grandpa asked as he and Milton walked toward us on the sidewalk.

"Ready to get it over with mostly," I groused.

"So, the plan is to start nice." Leighton hooked his arm in mine. "We're honest, not hiding anything, but we're nice. Jett and Allen will do most the talking."

Milton chuckled. "Me and Leighton are here for moral support. We can be called in for backup if needed."

"*And* to look pretty," Leighton teased. "Don't forget that part."

"*You* can look pretty," Milton retorted as we made our way up the steps to the front door. "And you do, by the way, you both look good."

Leighton beamed, his gray eyes sparkling. He'd gotten pastel pink, green, purple, blue, and yellow peek-a-boo stripes put in his hair and his gorgeous floppy blond mop was styled perfectly. A dangly earring, tight t-shirt, denim jacket, and skinny jeans with Cons completed his look for the evening.

Milton was right, my guy looked damn good.

I suddenly wanted to show him off.

For a split second, I let myself believe the night could possibly play out differently than I expected it would. Maybe Mom and Dad would see past what a disappointment I'd always been and just be glad I was happy. Maybe Leighton's pretty smile and sunshiny personality would melt their hearts the way it did mine.

Before I could even knock, the door swung open.

"What in God's name are you doing?" my mother hissed, stretching her neck to glance up and down the sidewalk. "Who are these men and why are you prancing up and down the sidewalk? Are you *trying* to make us the laughing stock of the neighborhood? My God, Jett, what in the world will people think?"

Any hope of my parents accepting me and coming to love Leighton the way I had went swirling down the drain.

"Get inside, now," Mom demanded.

The four of us made our way into the entryway, Leighton squeezing my hand tightly and Milton looking ready to fight anyone who even looked at Grandpa wrong.

"Dad, what's the meaning of this?" my father asked.

"Thought we were having dinner. Jett and I wanted to talk to you both. We brought some people who are very important to us." Grandpa put his arm around Milton in a defiant challenge.

"I didn't know you were bringing guests," Mom snipped, wrinkling her nose as if the air smelled bad. "Perhaps we should let your friends get back to whatever they were doing and have a *family* dinner."

"No worries, Mrs. Nelson," Leighton said with a friendly smile. "Milton and I have nothing else going on and we're thrilled to be here with Allen and Jett. You have a lovely home."

Mom stared at him, obviously torn between preening under the compliment and snapping back at the rest.

"Tom, Karen," Grandpa started. "We'd very much like if we could all sit down to a casual meal and chat—clear the air a bit. If that can't be done, we can speak here—or perhaps in the living room. Either way, your son and I have a bit to say and we aren't leaving until it's said."

"I, for one, am starving and think all conversations are best over a delicious meal," Leighton interjected.

My dad cleared his throat. "Perhaps we should have this conversation before we worry about dinner."

"Bummer," Leighton said. "Don't have anything delicious to serve?" he asked, his voice dripping with false sweetness.

I couldn't help my smile as I tucked him under my arm and kissed the top of his head. "No worries, we've got better places to be. Let's get this over with."

Mom sniffed and crossed her arms over her chest. "I think it's best if we just speak here."

"I figured as much," Grandpa said. "So, my grandson and I have been learning a lot about ourselves in the last several months. Last year, when I had a chainsaw accident—"

"What? We didn't know about that," Dad bit out.

"You know very little about me," Grandpa said. "Anyway, Milton and I have been friends for quite a while. He stepped in to help me during my recovery and the tiny sparks we'd been noticing between us turned into something more. Milton and I are in a relationship. We're not here for your blessing—we haven't been close for a very long time, if ever—but I wanted you to know about us because I won't hide who I really am."

Mom and Dad stared at Grandpa as if he'd grown three heads.

Milton squeezed Grandpa's hand quickly before sticking his hand out to shake. "Tom, Karen, it's nice to meet you." He chuckled humorlessly when they refused to reciprocate.

"And you?" Mom asked, wrinkling her nose as she glanced between Leighton and me. "Do you have something ridiculous to say as well?"

I took comfort in Leighton's arm wrapped around my waist. "Ridiculous? Nah, I'll leave that to Leighton."

My sunshiny boy beamed. "Hi, I'm Leighton. I'm in love with your son. Personally, after hearing about the way you treated him in the past and seeing how you're behaving tonight, I'd rather he flip you both the big ol' bird and never speak to you again. But because I love him, I'm here to support him in any way he needs. Because that's what you do when you love someone, you accept them and support them. You don't tell your own child they're a disappointment. You don't act as if you wish you'd had a different child altogether." He jutted his jaw and stared them down—I was actually surprised he hadn't said something inappropriate. "He doesn't need you. He has a family," Leighton gestured between the four of us, "he has a successful business, a great place to live, fabulous friends. You should consider yourselves lucky he's here to share his truth with you and offer you the chance to be in his life, because if I had my way, we'd be at home and he'd be fucking me into the mattress, making me scream his name." He leaned in and pretended to whisper, "This gay boy loves a good dicking."

And there it was.

Mom looked as if she was about to vomit and Dad was possibly going to stroke out, but Leighton wasn't done.

"Your son is the best person I've ever met and you'd

know that if you'd taken any time to actually know him. When he finally opens his heart to love, he loves with every ounce of his being. Your loss for never knowing that. But this little homo heart is happy to snatch up all that love and roll around in it like a pig in mud." He turned to murmur into my shoulder, "Okay, I think I'm done. Say what you need to say, your real family has dinner plans for pizza. Might even throw in a bit of gay porn." He batted his lashes at Mom and Dad. "You know, because that's what us damn homosexuals do, we ruin good people with porn. It's item seven on the gay agenda, or maybe it's eight."

I snorted. "Mom, Dad, this is Leighton. My boyfriend. If I have my way, he'll be my fiancé and husband in the future."

"Oh my god, dumplin', that's the sweetest thing I've ever heard," Leighton said. "Just so you know, don't ever be nervous to propose, I'm a sure thing."

I kissed him. "It'll happen, promise."

I turned back to my parents.

"I grew up thinking there was something wrong with me. I didn't make friends easily, had even more trouble keeping friends, dating girls felt wrong, but I never understood why. I was the outsider, the loaner, the bad boy just because I was quiet and serious and didn't fit in. And my own parents were just as bad as my peers." I clenched my fist, but relaxed when Leighton took my hand. "When I met Leighton, I thought he was just one more who would get tired of me and move on. But he didn't. He saw something in me and he didn't give up.

Thanks to him, I learned a lot about myself. I know I'm demisexual—I'm still figuring out if I'm gay or bisexual."

"Demi what? What does that even mean? Just another made-up label for attention probably," Mom huffed.

"It's not my responsibility to educate you. Look it up if you really want to know." I stood up straighter and took a cleansing breath. "All I know is I love Leighton with my entire heart—he's the first person, outside of Grandpa, to have given me a chance. He looked past the dark, quiet exterior and got to know the real me." I took another deep breath, every word leaving my mouth making me lighter and freer than I'd ever been. "I'd hoped coming here tonight could maybe start a road to healing and repairing our relationship, but I can see that's not going to happen. Ball's in your court. You want to have a relationship with your son, accept me for who I am. If not, it's your loss, I won't lose sleep over it. It took a while, but I've got real family and friends now." I put my arm around Leighton. "Come on, let's go have an actual family dinner."

The four of us walked out the door without a single backward glance. The sound of the door clicking closed behind us was exactly the closure I needed.

Grandpa and Milton held hands all the way to their parked vehicle as Leighton and I did the same and walked behind them.

I cleared my throat, breaking the silence which seemed to be more contemplative and serene than awkward and uncomfortable. "You still okay with driving us home?"

"Sure thing. And we're getting a couple pitchers of beer with our pizza in celebration of tonight. That felt damn good; I'm proud of you." Grandpa slapped me on the back.

That seemed to break Leighton out of his silence and he yapped the entire way to the pizza place about how awesome my words had been, how he loved me standing up to them, how their faces were priceless when he talked about sex—he didn't stop the whole ride and I couldn't hold back my smile as he spoke.

"You know I'll stand by you if they ever come around," Leighton said. "But know that you don't need them to. And if they do, you don't *owe* them anything after the way they've treated you."

"This is the best I've felt in my entire life. Telling them who I am, showing off the man I love, letting them know I'm okay without them—hell, better than okay, I'm great without them—it was a definite weight off my shoulders."

"Hey, what if we order a bunch of pizza and breadsticks, buy some beer, and head back to our place? I'm sure at least some of the gang is there and would be happy to help us celebrate on the rooftop," Leighton suggested.

"That sounds perfect," Milton said, he and Grandpa seemingly having their own silent conversation between hand holding and pointed looks. "I'm really proud of both of you, tonight was a big step."

Speaking to my parents and moving on *had* been a big step and I was grateful I'd taken it. But more than anything, I looked forward to all the next steps in my future. I had Leighton, my grandpa, my business, friends, and a true home—and I'd found it all on Cravenwood Block.

On Cravenwood Block continues with Ollie & Bash-
Find it HERE!
Visit A.D. Ellis's Amazon page for more!

Also by A.D. Ellis

Ollie & Bash: On Cravenwood Block- a steamy, opposites-attract, roommates-to-lovers, boss/employee, age-gap M/M romance featuring a man not looking for love and a younger music director with no filter.

Holly Hills Christmas- Holly Hills Christmas is a steamy, feel-good, M/M age-gap holiday romance.

The Perfect Blend- A steamy, M/M age-gap, marriage of convenience, coffee shop romance

Perfect Timing is a steamy, M/M romance with an introverted, demisexual writer and a big, soft teddy bear of a nurse trying to navigate a love they've always dreamed of but most definitely weren't expecting.

Adore (Remington Place 1) is a steamy, age-gap, bi-awakening, dad's best friend M/M romance with a sassy smartass and a sexy silver fox. It's the first book in the Remington Place series and can be read as a stand-alone.

Crave (Remington Place 2) is a steamy, friends-to-lovers, fake relationship M/M romance with a virgin nursing student and a gruff, grumbly construction worker.

Desire (Remington Place 3) is a steamy, age-gap, hurt/comfort M/M romance featuring a heart-of-gold mechanic and a twink who's a lot stronger than he realizes. *Please note: This story has mention of sex trafficking and sexual abuse.*

Yearn (Remington Place 4)- a steamy, enemies-to-lovers, forced proximity M/M romance between two EMS workers who have hated each other for a decade.

Power Struggle is a steamy M/M, age-gap, forced proximity

romance set in a small town. A twenty-year history, rival schools and jobs, and a hotel with only one bed make for a hot and heavy, sweet and sexy, HEA-guaranteed love story.

Take Me Home M/M age-gap, opposites-attract romance with plenty of steam and a scene that will make you appreciate camouflage and work boots

Let Love In M/M age-gap, forced proximity, dad's best friend, bisexual-awakening romance. Available on AUDIO!

Let Love Win M/M brother's best friend romance. Available on AUDIO!

Buried Secrets Romantic suspense stand-alone title. Available on AUDIO!

Silver in the City (3 books- meet the Silver crew you read about in Forged in the City) Available on AUDIO!

Forged in the City (3 books- a spin-off series from Silver in the City) Available on AUDIO

The BJ Boys Series (3 books, small town, big love) Available on AUDIO

Forever Better Together (friends to lovers) Available on AUDIO!

His Reluctant Cowboy (age gap, opposites attract, cowboy romance) Available on AUDIO!

What Blooms Beneath (LGBT Fantasy romance) Available on AUDIO!

Sawyer

(this was the first M/M I wrote and you may remember Sawyer and Luke being mentioned in Barrett & Ivan as well as in Ryker & Gavin)

———

The Something About Him series has been revamped with revised stories, updated blurbs, and spiffy new covers.

The series is available on ALL of your favorite book platforms!

Bryan & Jase

Brody & Nick

Barrett & Ivan

Braeton & Drew

Ryker & Gavin

Kade & Cameron

———

A.D.'s first stories (all male/female except <u>Sawyer</u> which is male/male) are in the Torey Hope and Torey Hope: The Later Years series. Find the 8 book box set HERE or you can find each individual title on Amazon.

For Nicky

Because of Beckett

Christmas in Torey Hope

Loving Josie

Decker

Sawyer

Zach

Kendrick

About the Author

A.D. Ellis is an Indiana girl, born and raised. She spends much of her time in central Indiana as an instructional coach/teacher in the inner city of Indianapolis, being a mom to two amazing teenagers, and wondering how she and her husband of over two decades haven't driven each other insane yet. A lot of her time is also devoted to phone call avoidance and her hatred of cooking.

She loves chocolate, wine, pizza, and naps along with reading and writing romance. These loves don't leave much time for housework, much to the chagrin of her husband. Who would pick cleaning the house over a nap or a good book? She uses any extra time to increase her fluency in sarcasm.

A.D. uses she/they pronouns.

Sign up at http://www.subscribepage.com/ADEllisNewsMMRomance for a FREE books!

Website http://adellisauthor.com/

Find me EVERYWHERE at https://www.adellisauthor.com/mylinks/

Connect with A.D. Ellis

Follow my website http://www.adellisauthor.com or find me on Facebook

http://www.facebook.com/adellisauthor

If you want to get updates about releases, interviews, sales, giveaways, and more please sign up for my newsletter http://www.subscribepage.com/ADEllisNewsMMRomance

Check out my TikTok- https://www.tiktok.com/@adellisauthor

You can also find me on Twitter http://www.twitter.com/ADEllisAuthor

Find me on Spotify if you'd like to listen to the playlist for this book (mainly just the songs I listened to while writing). Just search for A.D. Ellis.

To make it easy, find me EVERYWHERE here- https://www.adellisauthor.com/mylinks/

Acknowledgments

It's always so hard to write this part because I'm worried I'll forget someone without meaning to.

Readers- you are the reason I write. As long as you continue reading my stories, I'll continue writing them. Thank you for your support.

Bloggers- your support, reviews, and promotion are very much appreciated. Thank you!

My author buddies- I don't know that I could keep doing this without our brainstorm sessions, laughter, road trips, meals, wine, and friendship as my support.

Thank you to my alpha readers, betas, editors, proofreaders, and ARC readers! Your eyes and input are beyond important to me.

Brett and Gage- as usual, I doubt you even grasp how much your support, input, and friendship mean to me. This author journey has brought many wonderful things into my life, and you both are two of the BEST! I'm blessed to call you friends.

My family and friends- thank you for your love and support, always.